OZ TALES
PRESENTS

SHORT STORIES OF
MYSTERY
AND MURDER

Copyright © Short Stories of Mystery and Murder

FIRST EDITION: 2019
978-0-6485296-0-6 (hbk)
978-0-6485296-1-3 (pbk)
978-0-6485296-2-0 (e-bk)

The moral right of the author has been asserted.

Introduction © Chris Radge 2019
Beauty is in the Pie of the Beholder © Kaz Delaney
Bonnie and Clyde © Georgina Ballantine
Chemicals © Luke West
Date Night © Tania Cossich
Joe Vale's Last Case © Charmaine Clancy
Life's Not Perfect © Liane McDermott
Mile High © Martii Maclean
Murder On The Mountain © Paul Smith
Problem Solver © Kathy Childs
Smithy © Chris Radge
The Brisbane Strangler © Christine Childs
The One That Didn't Get Away © Lea Scott
Killer Bait © Diane K Edwards
The Phone Call © Anita Howard
Warning Labels © Kylie Thompson

Rainforest Writing Retreat is not responsible for websites (or their content) that are not owned by Rainforest Writing Retreat.

Cover and interior layout by the Self-Publishing Lab.

Contents

Introduction

Welcome to our Mystery and Murder tour, an anthology of fifteen new stories by RWR retreaters. This eclectic mix of tales will take you on a rollercoaster of emotion from heart-stopping terror to tears of joy with a touch of Australia. Demonstrating that, even with the most despicable of crimes, there's a method to the madness. I hope readers will find plenty to keep them entertained as they embark on this journey of Mystery and Murder.

The Rainforest Writing Retreat is a place where newbies and seasoned published writers meet each year. You will meet likewise thinking people, learn new techniques and get those ideas to finish your work in progress. If this sounds like something you're interested in, just go to www.rainforestwritingretreat.com and discover how to think, write, publish and promote straight from world-leading experts and best-selling authors in an immersive writing retreat experience.

Rainforest
Writing Retreat

Beauty is in the Pie of the Beholder

A Holly Hart Mystery

Kaz Delaney

The tension in the room was palpable. It throbbed and bounced off each contestant, swirling around them and twisting them into ever-tighter knots. Teeny droplets of sweat glistened off more than one brow, and sabre-sharp glances found their targets only to be returned with equally competitive hostility.

Pie baking was a lethal sport.

I shuddered. I'd been warned, but still, the Airlie Falls annual pie-baking competition had to be experienced to be believed. Competitors came from all over the county, and even the sweet, sugary aroma of fresh baking couldn't drown out the bitter smell of ill will.

A pat on the back here was likely to be accompanied by a knife. It would be adorned by a dainty ribbon and smeared with frosting, but a knife just the same.

Which was why I yelped when a hand touched my elbow. Two sets of eyes watched me pull myself together, all while I muttered some inane apology.

1

'Holly?'

Fiona was one of my closest friends and also the mother of my boyfriend, which could have been awkward but wasn't. She was also the wife of the mayor, which made her the first lady of tiny Airlie Falls, Texas, our hometown and host of this event. She was also the one who'd warned me that these bakers took themselves very seriously. And what a total understatement that was.

'Holly Hart,' Fiona continued, 'this is Gloria Lee Wiseman.'

The other woman didn't return my smile and I decided there was nothing glorious about Gloria Lee Wiseman. Her pointed features reminded me of a meerkat, and something about her eyes pushed me to the conclusion that the surname Wiseman wasn't a true indication of her character. Rat-cunning would have been closer.

She took hold of my extended hand with just the tips of her fingers. 'Holly Hart?' she repeated in a drawl I recognised as Australian. 'Aren't you that girl who solved all those murders?'

My eyes darted to Fiona, who was having trouble containing her laughter. I mean, yes, I was 'that girl', but the tone Gloria Lee had used made it sound like I had actually committed the murders rather than solved them. Sad, really. My experience with Australians had led me to believe that they were laidback, fun people. Gloria Lee was obviously the exception.

'Helped,' I corrected quietly. '*Helped* solve a couple of murders.'

She sniffed, pointing that sharp little nose northwards, and added a helpless miniscule shake of her head. It spoke volumes; she was in the presence of something slightly dirty and distasteful.

I didn't even try to hide my eyeroll. 'Don't worry, Gloria Lee, I'm sure there'll be nothing as common as a murder here at the pie competition.'

A movement to the right caught my eye; two big-bosomed women were facing off. All they needed were their rolling pins. On second thoughts ...

Turning back to Gloria Lee, I found her glaring at me and hastened to lighten the situation. After all, we were the hosts of this event and it was our job to make everyone feel comfortable, most especially an overseas guest. Donning my best—which is very bad—Sam Spade imitation, I leaned in close in a show of mock conspiracy.

'Although I hear the chief judge isn't very popular, so I can't actually guarantee there won't be bloodshed. You know what I mean? Some of these bakers look like they're ready to crack. Who'd be a judge, right?' I finished on a chuckle. It took me a moment longer to realise neither of the other two had joined me.

That's when that horrid stomach-sinking feeling took over. I knew what Fiona was going to say before she'd even uttered a word. Gloria Lee's expression was the clue.

'Holly dear, I should have added that Gloria Lee is the long-standing chief judge of the pie-baking competition. She flies in each year for the event.'

Gloria Lee said nothing as she stomped away, but if looks could kill, I'd have been today's victim. I watched her determined strides as she pushed rudely through the crowd, watched her outsize bag bump heavily against her generous hip. I didn't need to see her face. The bumping provided the tone and rhythm for her anger: hard, unwavering and unforgiving.

Maybe she just had jet lag.

Wishful thinking.

Internally, I shrugged. I guessed I could say goodbye to a free bed or any recommendations if ever I visited Australia. I'd probably find a redback spider in the bed. Or were they just on toilets?

I had to face it. I'd made an enemy. And she was a baking judge, no less. Not that it would affect the outcome of the day's proceedings. I hadn't entered the competition, so I wasn't fearful of upsetting a judge. My bakery business, From the Hart, could certainly have benefited from a win, but I felt that my semi-professional status might be viewed as an unfair advantage so I'd volunteered to be on the committee instead.

'Don't worry about her,' Fiona whispered. 'Sadly, everything you said is true. She's not liked; she's got a track record of reducing contestants to tears with her scathing critiques. Besides, it's time to clear this main room for the blind judging. That's where she'll be right in her element. She won't be giving you a second thought.'

It happened almost exactly like that. The fifty or so competitors and audience members were ushered into an anteroom in the community centre, which was roughly the same size as the judging room. Only the chief judge and her secondary judge were allowed to remain with the pies.

Refreshments were served to those waiting, but it seemed only those who didn't have an entry had an appetite. Those who did hovered nervously, usually in the centre of their support group, who bounced around the competitor like boxers' seconds, anticipating the contestants' every need.

The clock ticked slowly. At thirty-seven minutes in, all faces turned to a sound coming from the judging room. And even though this was my first county pie-baking competition, even I knew the sound wasn't what anyone expected.

It was a scream, a long, bloodcurdling scream. A scream that pierced the psyche of every person waiting, and for a second I wondered which pie had been that bad.

Then the fog cleared.

First everyone remained frozen, and then the stampede began. Fiona, being tall and sturdy, forced her way to the front, with me right behind her. We found Mara Standish, the bird-like sixty-year-old secondary judge, leaning over the prone body of Gloria Lee Wiseman.

'She's dead! She's dead! I just slipped out for a moment and I came back and found her *dead*.'

A flurry of voices floated around me. Shock and disbelief were the loudest sentiments, and yet there was something off about the deliveries. The closest one reached me in a quivery voice.

'Oh, no, I can't believe it. Poor Gloria Lee. Such a wonderful woman, God rest her soul.'

Muted voices added their agreement.

Fiona wrapped her arms around Mara while I knelt beside the victim. Gloria Lee was lying partly under the pie-display table. Shards of smashed china and food crumbs surrounded her body, especially her head. The shards of china were probably part of the weapon—plate—that had rendered her unconscious. A small trickle of blood stained her bleached-blonde hair and dripped onto the white tile flooring.

The crowd moved closer. I placed my finger at the side of her neck and, confused, raised my hand to ask for silence. As one, the group quieted and I lowered my face to Gloria Lee's face. When I shook my head, several in the closest rows gasped, and either placed hands on their hearts or raised them to their mouths in an unspoken act of grief.

Until I spoke. 'She's not dead.'

The woman who'd asked God to rest Gloria's soul froze with her hand midway to her mouth. This time her voice was firm and sharp. 'What? What do you mean she's not dead? Are you sure? Check again. Surely you're mistaken.'

'No, I'm not mistaken. She's not dead. And we need the paramedics.'

Other voices drifted to me.

'Not dead?'

'Oh, gimme a break!'

'Who said she's not dead? What kind of a nasty trick was that? She *must* be dead.'

The reaction of the crowd startled me a bit. Accusing faces glared at me, and I knew how the targets of lynch mobs felt. Wow. Fiona hadn't been wrong when she said Gloria Lee was disliked.

The strength of their sentiments was even more clear seconds later when yet another scream filled the room.

'What's happening?' someone from the back called. 'Is she dead this time?'

'My pie! My beautiful pie!'

A space cleared and I could see the problem. A pie— and not just any pie; the pie of the woman tipped to take out the trophy and bragging rights again—was splattered over the floor just to the side of us in a congealing mess of golden pastry, apple, and ruby-red raspberries that rippled through the puddle like coagulating blood clots. And this time the gasps of shock and horror were genuine.

Joanna Garcia. The baker's name came to me as I tried to assess if Gloria Lee had any other injuries.

I remembered Joanna's pie before it had been pulped; I had been impressed. Presentation was part of the criteria, and her pastry had been an intricate layering of individually cut leaves fanning out from the centre. At that centre, she'd tinted a couple of the pastry leaves with green colouring and they in turn cupped a grouping of glazed berries.

And that wasn't all. It was presented on the top layer of a double cake stand, and below on the bigger plate were stacked at least a dozen and a half miniature pies that were identical to the main entry. The miniature pies were

7

displayed on a bed of greenery, and sprigs of berries were entwined through the pies. It had been quite stunning.

My eyes met Fiona's.

'I've called Frank, but he's at least an hour away,' she said, tilting her phone toward me.

Police Chief Frank Kinnead was one of the fairest men I'd ever met: ethical and with integrity to spare, but more importantly, a man who possessed loads of common sense. Nearing retirement age, Frank had protected the town of Airlie Falls for most of his adult life. He also disliked me poking my nose into his cases, but only for my own safety. Not that it ever stopped me.

Ascertaining that Gloria Lee wasn't in any further danger that we knew of, I stood and moved to Mara Standish, shuffling her and Fiona out of earshot of the hovering crowd. 'Mara, can you tell us what exactly happened?'

She nodded. Between sobs, she said, 'It was the lemon cream pie. It was so sticky and, well, we worried that the stickiness would interfere with our tastings and I went to get some wet wipes. I wasn't gone long, but, well, you know, maybe a lot longer than I should have because someone had put them in the wrong place in the centre's kitchen. It took me ages to find them and it made me mad because we're quite strict about things going straight back into their correct places and Gloria Lee would have been angry if I hadn't found them and ...'

I nodded, gently bringing her back on track, trying not to be distracted by the growing buzz from the crowd behind me.

'Oh,' she said, getting more flustered, 'I'm sorry. I just, well, it was such a shock.'

Again I nodded, encouraging her to continue.

'It was the open exterior door I saw first. Or felt, at least. The wind was rushing in and it was chilly. I couldn't imagine who had opened it, but I wasn't worried about that. All I wanted to do was close the darned thing before I froze.'

'And then?'

'Well, I turned to come back up to the judging area and that's when I saw her. Just lying there. And I thought ... I thought ...' The sobbing started anew and Fiona rocked her, like you'd rock a child. 'And, oh my gosh, then I saw that pie. Such a beautiful thing, and just *ruined*.'

For a moment it seemed she was more upset over the pie than by Gloria Lee's assault. I pushed that thought aside.

Fiona said, 'Mara, are you saying you didn't hear anything?'

Mara looked up at Fiona. 'I saw nothing and I heard nothing.'

A flurry of movement broke up our tête-à-tête. The paramedics arrived and started working on Gloria Lee. At the same time, a friend of Mara's pushed through with a hot drink, insisting that she have something to help calm her.

Fiona nudged us even further away from the others. 'What do you think is happening here?' she said. 'This is all a bit extreme just to push Joanne Garcia out of the running, don't you think?'

I agreed. 'But she does seem to be some sort of target.' My mind was racing. 'Was the door between us and the judges locked?'

.

9

Fiona shrugged. 'It isn't usually. I mean, these people take this very seriously; the bragging rights carry a lot of weight around the county. Some winners have had television appearances and everything. One got a show on the food network.'

'So if someone was desperate they could have come in and ...' I shook my head. 'It doesn't make sense. Whoever did that would surely know that they'd be seen.'

'Which is obviously what happened,' Fiona added. 'They sneaked in, Gloria Lee caught them, and to keep her quiet they bopped her on the head.'

I was still struggling with that, even though it seemed to be the logical answer. 'What about the open door, the one leading outside? Someone could have come in that way, either a contestant or someone working for them, but who?' My eyes scanned the crowd. 'Let's talk to Joanne.'

We pulled Joanne Garcia into a quiet, makeshift interrogation corner, and her eyes flashed. 'You want me to name anyone who wanted me to fail? Are you crazy? Every person in this room wanted me to fail. I was odds-on to win this competition. I won the combined churches competition last month, and the Huber Elementary School competition the month before. They're like the Golden Globes, and this is the Oscars. Whoever wins those is the favourite to win this one.'

After five full minutes describing how great and deserving she was, Joanne finally gave us a name and we moved her on.

Dee Dee Swift moved like a snail. Why was I so focused on the suitability of names this evening?

'Dee Dee,' I said, 'you were seen hovering very close to the door separating the judging area from the waiting area during judging. Did you happen to come into the judging room?'

'Of course I didn't.' Her multiple chins added their outrage, continuing to wobble long after she'd ceased shaking her head. 'Did that meanie Joanne say that? Well, let me tell you something.'

'Please,' I said, with little enthusiasm.

'I think Joanne planned this herself. That's what I think.'

'Because ...' Fiona prompted.

'Because she knew she wasn't going to win, that's why. She admitted that she didn't think this pie was as good as her others that had won before, and she was afraid she wouldn't win. So, rather than face that humiliation, she sabotaged her own pie.' Tears filled her eyes. 'That poor pie. How could she do that? How could she even think it?'

For my own sanity I ignored the last outburst. 'Did she actually admit she was going to do that? Sabotage the pie?'

Dee Dee looked down. 'Well, not to me, but I'm sure Sarah Connell knows.'

Sarah Connell was self-appointed pie security. 'There was a whisper,' she admitted. 'But I brushed it of as jealous mutterings. Besides, it would never happen. No pie was going to be lost tonight. Not on my watch.'

We chose not to remind her that a pie had indeed been 'lost', and went on to the name she gave up.

And so it went, as entrant after entrant dobbed in their fellow contestants. All we got out of that—besides the fact that most of them had had one too many sniffs of the vanilla bottle—was that Joanne had a secret ingredient that put her pastry way above the rest, and everybody wanted it. And if they couldn't have it, they were going to pull her down some other way. But, sadly, everyone had witnesses that swore that none of them had entered the judging room.

Most of all, we got the message that while they'd take each other out without blinking an eye, pies were sacred. The fact that someone had destroyed the pie was a shock they couldn't fathom. It was like they'd sworn an oath to protect the pie at all costs: the Mounties of the pie-baking world.

I sighed and accepted the coffee Fiona handed me. 'I think we have to go back to considering that Gloria Lee was the target, not the pie.'

Her glance swept the room. 'Either way, we have a room full of suspects.'

Fiona had dealt with the paramedics, who were now leaving with Gloria Lee on a gurney. She handed me a baggie with a small piece of china inside. 'They said to give this to Frank. Apparently it was clutched in her left hand.'

Idly I turned it over, looking at it from both sides. 'I wonder how it got to be in her hand.' Scenarios turned over slowly in my mind. 'Did she grasp it as she went down? Was she conscious on the ground for a moment and reached out to find something to help herself?'

'The head paramedic,' Fiona said carefully, 'told me he's pretty sure she'd have been out to it almost immediately. Oh, and she'd had one of those small pies. There was residue in her mouth and crumbs inside her blouse.'

'Did the paramedic say anything else?'

She nodded. 'Yes, that she was unlucky to have been hit where she was. Most times a whack like this wouldn't have knocked someone unconscious, but the angle was strange and it just got her on the right—or wrong—spot.'

'Weird,' I said, shaking my head. 'Let's look more closely at where she fell.'

Everyone had given that area a wide berth. There was no chalk outline, but there may as well have been. Pies were strewn everywhere, interspersed with broken china fragments. Suddenly the scene looked different.

More importantly, something was missing.

Pushing everyone even further back, I scoured the floor and the table, even under the table, which was where it all came together for me. One teeny item I found went into my jeans pocket. Yep, we were on the right track.

'Fiona, can you find me an old plate?'

She came rushing back with one from the kitchen while I was still examining the mess. Taking it, I shrugged. 'We're going to have to break this.' A few nervous screams accompanied the smash, which I ignored. I was way more interested in the result.

'Look at this, Fiona,' I said, 'it's a clean break. Just three pieces and a few teeny shards.'

She frowned. 'This plate of Joanne's must have been very old, then, because it smashed into a million pieces. It's barely even recognisable as a plate.'

'I think that's the point exactly,' I said, with a grin. 'Well done, Sherlock.'

While she frowned at me like I'd lost my marbles, I called Mara over. 'Could I see your bag, please?'

Her puffy eyes widened. 'Why?'

'Please, just humour me.'

Huffing, she led me to where she'd stashed her bag in a corner near the outer door.

I gave it a cursory glance. 'Was Gloria Lee's here as well?'

Flustered, she looked around the area, now empty apart from her own bag. 'Of course it was. It was her suggestion we put them here, way out of harm's way.'

Next, I called Joanne over again. She wasn't looking any happier.

'I've been hearing that you think I did this myself,' she said. 'Well, I can assure you—'

'Joanne, I'd rather talk about the plate you chose to display your pies on. Can you describe it?'

She shrugged, teaming it with a look that told me she thought I was crazy. 'Well, it was a double-tiered cake stand. I picked it up at a flea market a few weeks back. It had some kind of floral design and a gold trim. It didn't have a top handle so it was perfect for the pie. That's when I got the idea to make the small ones for the plate underneath.'

'Did you tell anyone about the plate?'

Again she shrugged. 'I put a photo up on Facebook. It was such a cute plate and it only cost me a few dollars, a bargain.'

Out of the corner of my eye I saw the dawning look of comprehension cross Fiona's face and she dived for her phone, no doubt to connect to Facebook, I thought.

Meanwhile, I picked up a piece of china. 'Does this look like a piece of it?'

She stared closely. 'I'm not sure. It's hard to tell, it's so tiny.'

Fiona caught my eye and nodded. 'Bag?'

I nodded back and she took off toward the other end of the room. Before she returned, Police Chief Frank Kinnead lumbered in, looking tired and a bit grumpy. Not good.

'Hey, Chief,' I said.

He scowled. 'I hope you haven't been poking your nose in, Holly Hart.'

Slightly puffed, Fiona appeared back at my side. 'Indeed she has, Frank Kinnead, and you'd better listen. I think she's saved you a whole heap of effort.' This was delivered in her best Texas first-lady voice and he knew better than to argue. If he didn't, he'd only cop it from his wife later anyway.

'As a matter of fact, Holly darlin',' Fiona continued, 'I think you'd better tell us all. Nice and loud so we can hear.'

Heat suffused my face as I took a moment to compose myself and ensure that I was on the right track. 'Well, if I've got this right, only one person could have hit Miss Gloria Lee on the head tonight and that was ...' My eyes wandered the room; some people some squirmed, others looked anxious. Mara Standish looked terrified.

'It wasn't me, Holly,' she said. 'I know I was the only one here—'

'It's okay, Mara. You didn't do it, and you weren't the only one here. There was one other person.'

'Who?' someone called out.

'Gloria Lee Wiseman herself.'

As I expected, mayhem broke out. I held up a hand. 'Gloria Lee had this planned down to the last detail. The only thing that went wrong was that she hit herself too hard and had to be carted off to hospital.'

I turned to Fiona. 'Did you look at the Facebook entry?'

'Yes, I did, and I'm a bit of an amateur, but I've got a good idea. That plate you got was indeed a bargain, Joanne. If I'm correct—and given Gloria Lee's elaborate plan, I think I am—that plate is worth a fortune.'

More mayhem broke out.

'But why did she smash it then?'

'That's just plain mean.'

I held up my hand once more. 'That's the thing, she didn't. She stole it. And here's what I think happened. 'I think Gloria Lee saw the plate on Facebook, recognised it and had to have it. Mara, the place she chose for your bags was deliberate, right near the outer doors. And the reason you couldn't find the wipes? She put them somewhere obscure, knowing you'd have to search. You see, she needed time for her plan, which was to make it seem like someone had come in the back door and smashed Joanne's pie display, including the plate. Hitting herself on the head was to make her seem like the innocent victim, and also help when she couldn't "remember" who burst through the door.'

Frank was shaking his head. 'And what, Miss Holly, made you come up with this elaborate story?'

I ignored his scepticism. 'Four things. One, the plate was more smashed up than the pies. As Fiona said, it was almost unrecognisable as a plate. That struck me as odd. Second, Mara didn't hear anything. She didn't hear the plate smash. To me, that meant it arrived at the scene already smashed, probably in a baggie. The third thing was the giveaway. The plate was a two-tiered model. That meant there should have been a centre support rod, and there wasn't. I searched.'

'You said four things,' Joanne called.

'Yes, fourth was the piece of plate in her hand. If she'd been hit with it, how did it get into her hand? But I guess it's the last one. So, five clues in all, and that seals the deal.' I paused. 'I'm pretty sure Gloria Lee whacked her head, deliberately, on the underside of the table. Not by hitting herself with a plate.'

Frank's eyes were narrowed now, and his mouth had that kissy look I knew was his thinking pose. He was seeing the sense of this. 'I don't suppose you have any proof of this.'

I pointed to Fiona, who handed over Gloria Lee's outsize bag. Frank took it and lifted out two plates in a bag along with a centre rod.

'I found it stashed under a bush out by the back door,' Fiona said.

17

'And I don't know if this is a clue for you, but it was for me.' Digging into my pocket, I pulled out the teeny screw I found on the table near where the pie display had stood. 'She must have dropped it when she took the plate apart.'

Frank's eyes were still on me as I said, 'And I think if you check under the table, Frank, you'll see where she cracked her head. There's fresh blood there.'

Frank said nothing as he checked, then he packed up everything he needed, replaced the Stetson he'd removed when he came into the room and headed for the door. 'Holly, I'll talk to you tomorrow. Right now I need to talk to a certain lady at the hospital.'

I stared after him. There was one plus, I supposed. I wasn't going to worry about the loss of one potential Aussie connection, or the offer of a bed. Even if Gloria Lee was extradited, I still saw a cold, narrow cot in her future. And I figured the boys in blue might object to her inviting overnight guests, to say nothing of her 'interesting' roommates.

Fiona sighed, pulling me out of my reverie. There was a quiet buzz floating around the room. I got it; there was a lot to comprehend.

'All this over a plate,' she said quietly. 'And here we thought it was sabotage or revenge or hatred.'

'Nah, just plain greed,' I said. 'One of the least interesting of the seven sins.'

Laughing, she hooked her arm through mine. 'You know this means we're going to need a new judge.' There was a definite question in that comment.

Carefully I unhooked my arm and glanced around the room. Images appeared of grandmothers and mothers and sisters, and dads and brothers, all baking pies through the ages. Of rosy cheeks and floured aprons. Of smiling children playing with pastry and crafting sugarcoated mystery shapes to bake and eat. Of spilled sugar and warm kitchens. Of antique rolling pins and steaming bowls of sweetened fruit. Of the love and pride that inspires each pie.

My heart softened ... until a muffled scream to my left dumped me squarely back in the heart of reality.

A woman was dripping in berry pie, which clashed violently with her orange jumpsuit and matching hair. The woman standing in front of her was about to be adorned with strawberry meringue. A much better coupling, I thought: she was wearing hot pink.

I glanced back at Fiona. 'Are you kidding? I value my life way too much.'

Bonnie and Clyde

Georgina Ballantine

Clyde Barrow woke to brain freeze. A translucent figure hovered above him, one exploratory finger buried deep between Clyde's eyes. Rolling to the side, Clyde shuddered as the finger slid from his head like an icy pole through jello.

The naked spirit's mean, thin face seemed familiar. Clyde grinned. 'Buck, ol' buddy, great to see ya. Bin a long time. But keep yer hands to yerself, all right?' He hopped out the other side of the bed, threw on a white cotton bathrobe and turned to face the apparition.

'Now hang on, Buck, 'cause I'm tryin' to remember how Bonnie did this for me.' He took a deep breath, running his fingers through his limp, chestnut hair. 'Yer name is Marvin Ivan Barrow, but we've always called ya Buck. I'm Clyde, and yer my big brother. An' the year's 2018, October.'

He studied the ghost's confused expression. 'Ah, sod it. Yer dead, brother, a puff of smoke, will o' the wisp, all waft and no weight. Got the back of yer head smashed in, remember? No? Bin gone for round eighty-five years, just like me. But now yer back.'

Buck's narrow eyes widened; he looked at his hands and then waved them through his crotch. A strangled gasp escaped the gape of his mouth.

Clyde chuckled. 'Yeah, bud, I checked the family jewels, too. Don't blow yer wig, they're comin' back. Me an' Bonnie bin givin' mine a right ol' workout, know what I mean?'

He winked at the ghost.

Buck stared back blankly.

Clyde shrugged. 'Ah, well, you'll figure it out, Buck. Took me 'bout two days to git my head round bein' in the future. Park yerself over there, on that there fancy chair, and I'll call up Bonnie. She'll know what to do. I'll be back in a minute to fill in the gaps. Some of them, anyways.'

He watched Buck drift over to an embroidered chaise longue, his angular face twisting from side to side as he took in his surroundings. Clyde stifled a guffaw when Buck tried to sit but instead sank slowly through the elaborate fabric, shooting back up to float above it.

Chuckling, Clyde sauntered through to the kitchen, yawned and lit up a Camel. He grabbed his mobile from the counter, hitting speed dial #1. 'Bonnie? Hey, doll, got a situation here. Yeah, it's Buck. Ya better git back here, 'case he loses it.'

He ended the call, tossing the phone back on the counter. 'What the hell is that creepy Moll broad playin' at, bringin' back Buck on us?' he muttered. 'Thought it was jus' gonna me be an' the missus.'

He forced a cheerful grin onto his face, grabbed a miniature JD from the bar fridge and strode back into the bedroom.

Bonnie Parker knew when she had a good thing going. She'd known it back in '33, on that cold winter's morning

21

at 105 Herbert St, West Dallas, when Clyde sauntered uninvited into the parlour. She'd known it when he'd swept her heart away with that devilish smile, when she'd smuggled the pistol into prison to help him escape, and, gun in hand, they'd made love under the stars. Sure, they'd ended up dead only three years later, but what a fine time they'd had till the coppers'd shot the shit out of them.

Now, though, everything felt unconnected. This world of 2018 was … unbalanced. Paranoia hung about the people she watched who, day and night, stared at their screens. They seemed sharp: aware, but afraid. Sure, those she spoke to made conversation, sometimes joked around, but she sensed the tension in their movements, their interactions. What had happened to humanity to cause this deep mistrust?

Today was no different. She had driven the Porsche to the bank, like Moll had told her to, tracking the coppers and security guards while Clyde slept off their lovemaking. When Clyde had called, she'd left the car and hurried on home in one of those grotesque but fast yellow cabs. The drivers always asked her where she was from and what she was doing in Manhattan; she enjoyed playing dumb, spinning elaborate stories in her East Texas drawl. Tales that made the drivers shut up fast, thinking they had a crazy on their hands.

Now, as she waited for the lift to take her to level five of the downtown Sheraton, the phone rang. She sighed at the caller ID.

'Hi there, Moll,' she said, rolling her eyes. 'Yeah, I'm peachy. Tomorrow? But … but we ain't ready. Dammit, Moll. Yes, Buck's arrived. I'm headin' back now to help transition him. Wish you'd told me he was comin', though. Clyde an' me, we thought we'd be workin' this alone. Buck's an intense kinda guy. But Moll, not tomorrow. Please, we jus' can't.'

The high, childish voice at the other end of the line prattled on about strategies, entry points and times.

Bonnie chewed her lip. How in god's name did Moll expect them to pull off this heist? Images of the rifles Moll had left in their room overnight flashed through her mind. Ammo-heavy automatic weapons; guns that didn't miss. Oh, she was learning every day, and what she discovered made her want to run straight back to the grave. If it weren't for Clyde, she'd have topped herself by now for sure.

Moll ended the conversation the way she always did, telling her that 'Bonnie and Clyde were the most awesome criminals in history', that she was their 'greatest fan', and that this was their chance to 'relive their glory days'. Had Moll thought the same about the other dead crims she'd brought back before her and Clyde?

God, but Bonnie needed a cigarette. Back in the old days, when she wanted a smoke she goddamn took one, wherever and whenever. But this hotel had detector things stuck everywhere that whined each time she lit up. At least Clyde had ripped out the ones in the hotel room. She gritted her teeth, digging her fingernails into her palms until they bit hard into her soft flesh.

Outside room 501, Bonnie slipped her key card inside the slot and pushed on the heavy door.

'That you, doll?' Clyde yelled from the shower.

'Sure is, Clyde,' she said, her gaze sweeping the empty whiskey bottles strewn across the kitchen counter. 'Ya got Buck in there, too? Having a reunion?'

The water stopped. Clyde emerged from the bedroom, hair wet and a towel around his waist. God, but he was handsome. If it weren't for the tall, swarthy man making his careful way towards her from across the lounge, she'd have whipped that towel off Clyde in a tenth of a second.

'Buck,' she said, giving him her best smile. 'How the devil are ya?' She prodded at Buck's pinkish arm to see if he was solid enough to hug. His skin felt spongy, but it held. 'Ah, yer still cookin', but yer wearin' pants already so it won't be long now. Took Clyde maybe two hours to git himself all back together.'

Buck frowned. He raised one hand, pointed at her, Clyde and himself, and then gestured at the windows with a quizzical expression.

Bonnie raised an eyebrow at Clyde. 'Have ya told him anythin', Clyde? Or ya jus' bin taking skinfuls of that there whiskey while Buck here wonders what in hellfire's goin' on?'

Clyde grinned and grabbed her around the waist. 'Woman, don't ya go tellin' me not to take a drink when I need one. Ya used to knock 'em back good and proper in our day. Ain't no temperance folk round here, far's I can tell. No need for me to lay off like I used to.'

He crushed Bonnie's lips against his, then slapped her behind and turned to Buck. 'Hey, brother, take a look at this.' He bent down to open the mini bar. 'Ev'ry type of liquor a man could wish for. They still got the kid-size bottles, jus' like back when. But I seen stores on ev'ry corner here in New York City full of hooch a mile high. They gonna blow yer mind, brother.'

Bonnie laughed. 'Okay, boys, let's git down to business, now. Sit on over there, Clyde, an' you, if ya can, Buck.'

The air-conditioning whirred and buzzed in the background as Clyde and Buck made their way over to the voluminous sofas, Buck's feet now connecting with the carpet. Bonnie picked up the remote and switched on the TV.

'So as no one can hear us,' she said, winking at Buck, whose eyes flicked between hers and the bright colours of *Sesame Street*.

Bonnie grabbed a newspaper from a magazine rack and tossed it in front of them. Three pairs of eyes fixed on the headlines.

BABYFACE GOT BACK!
Lookalike heist number three and counting.

'This here's what it's all about, Buck,' Bonnie said, sliding down next to Clyde. 'Babyface George Nelson and John Dillinger, remember them? They died, year after us, back in thirty-four. Only one week back, they done robbed a bank over in Queens. The week before, Bugs Moran stole a heap of cash from the tills down in Brooklyn, and before him, Jesse James an' his gang. Yep, ya heard me. There's this broad, Moll, got some voodoo in her or somethin', bin resurrectin' us crims to go make her a bunch of dough, an' we git to keep a share.'

Buck was looking at her like she was nuts, the same way Clyde had when she'd tried to explain it to him. Ah well, he'd believe her soon enough.

25

'Imagine that, Buck,' said Clyde, propping his feet up on the coffee table, 'a ton of long greens, all for the keepin'. Dough doesn't buy as much as it did in our day, but Bonnie says we'll have enough to cruise the Caribbean. I'm thinkin' we could buy us a yacht an' sail all the way to Australia. Bonnie's always wanted to see one of them kangaroos hoppin' about, ain't ya, Bon?'

Buck exploded into a fit of coughing, and Bonnie fetched him a glass of water. 'There now, Bucky,' she crooned, rubbing his back. 'Should mean yer pipes are workin' again'. Try an' say a few words, go on.'

Buck cleared his throat and looked straight at Bonnie. 'Where's Blanche? Where's my goddamn wife?'

Bonnie's face creased with concern and she frowned at Clyde, who evaded her gaze. 'Ya ain't told him, Clyde? Well, that's just swell.'

'Didn't think as he could take it,' Clyde mumbled. He lit a cigarette and prodded at his mobile screen, ignoring Bonnie's glare.

Bonnie sighed and took Buck's hand in hers, feeling his restored warmth and strength. 'Buck, darlin', Blanche lived a while longer than us. They sent her to prison, but not for more than a few years. She died in 1988, Buck, and, well, she got hitched again. Some fella named Eddie.'

Buck stared at Bonnie, then at Clyde. He inhaled a wheezy, lung-filling breath that sounded like a punctured bagpipe. 'Damn broad,' he yelled. Grabbing a bottle of Wild Turkey from the table, he took a long swig. He shrugged. 'I don't bloody well care. She can rot in hell.' He hurled the bottle at the wall. Whiskey and shards of glass exploded over the carpet, sending a sour, volatile scent through the room.

Bonnie laid a calming hand on Buck's arm, but he shook her off, jabbing a finger at the newspaper. 'So, ya sayin' some nuts dame brought us back to pull off a job? Why us? Ain't they got their own goons in 2018?'

'Yeah, Buck. They got crims an' goons aplenty,' Clyde said, lighting up a Camel. 'Ya want one, Buck, ol' boy?' Buck shook his head. 'Yeah, jus' read that there paper. Crims all over, but they ain't expendable like us dead 'uns. The boss made that clear. We git shot, we jus' fade away. No ID, no murder charge, no heat for her. The deal is, we git in there an' steal the dough, take twenty percent then stash the rest for her. Then she lets us live the life of Riley wherever the hell we want to hang our hats.'

A tentative knock sounded at the door.

Bonnie frowned at Buck. 'Ya go 'round smashin' bottles an' security'll kick us out. An' Clyde, put out that cigarette, right now.' She walked to the door and opened it a crack. A tiny, smiling girl in a blue-striped overall stood before her, no more than sixteen, she guessed.

'I am sorry to disturb you,' the girl whispered in a lightly accented voice as diminutive as herself. 'I am Angelique, your housekeeping maid. Is everything okay? I heard loud noises.'

'Yeah, it's all fine, Angelica. Thanks for checkin' up on us now. Bye.' Bonnie tried to close the door, but the maid pushed back with surprising strength.

27

'It's Angelique, and please, no more noise.' She shook her head, beaded braids clattering. 'People will complain. They will call *sécurité*.'

Bonnie raised one eyebrow at the delicate girl, who looked as if a short bout of vacuuming would break her in half. 'Yes, Angelica, got it. No more noise,' and she pushed the door shut, hard.

Turning, she felt a familiar twist inside her stomach, the feeling she always had when something wasn't right. 'Clyde, I think that maid's spyin' on us,' she said, frowning. 'And Buck, keep the ruckus down. Yer gonna git us found out.'

Clyde shrugged, but Buck sank his head into his hands. 'Ya got some crazy booshwa goin' on. Who's runnin' the heists?'

Bonnie picked up a cushion, pulling on the spare threads, trying to sound nonchalant. 'Her name's Moll, but I haven't ever met her. She talks to me on this.' She held up her mobile for Buck to see. 'It's a telephone. Yeah, I know. Hard to buy, ain't it? But yeah, ya can call up anyone on this bit of glass an' metal. Anyhow, Moll say she's the one that brought us back to life, and she'll stick us right back there in the dirt if we don't cooperate.'

Buck looked from Bonnie to Clyde, pulling at the loose flap of skin beneath his chin. 'I bin looking out the window, brother. Cars everywhere, so fast I can't believe everyone ain't goddamn dead like us. An' yer tellin' me everyone has a telephone in their coat pocket?' He swung around, pointing at the TV. 'An' there's things goin' on in that there box of talkin', movin' pictures I don't understand. Ya gonna need to give me time to git my brain 'round this, brother. Ya gonna need to give me time.'

'Yeah, okay, Buck.' Bonnie sniffed, checking her fingernails. 'Hey, Clyde baby, I jus' spoke with Moll. This heist is goin' down tomorrow.'

Bonnie was sitting at the kitchen counter with a strong cup of Joe when Clyde and Buck rolled in at midnight, singing 'All of Me' by Louis Armstrong. The bank's floor plans and Manhattan street maps lay in front of her, and she scribbled endless notes on hotel notepaper.

As the men sang and staggered, memories surrounded her: Clyde serenading her on a humid, summer evening. They were on the run, sleeping out by the river and he'd cradled her face in his hands, swearing to love her always. Now here she sat, in the year 2018, looking at her fiance. Nothing could stop them getting married now; her jailbird husband Roy must be long dead. Love burned inside her with a determination so fierce that she knew she'd do anything to stay with him. Anything that Moll wanted.

Just eleven hours later, Bonnie and Clyde burst through the hotel door, dropping their guns and a large, black leather bag in the foyer.

'Woohoooo!' whooped Bonnie, kicking the door shut. She wrapped her arms around her lover and pulled him back towards the sofa. Clyde laughed and closed his mouth over hers. Bonnie started to pull at his pants, but he stopped her.

'Hey, wild Sheba, we gotta clean up and git outta here. Coppers'll be onto us real soon.'

29

Bonnie pouted, but let go. 'Yeah, yer right. At least they won't find no trace of Buck.' Her eyes softened. 'I'm sorry, Clyde. I don't know how he got hit 'cause I didn't hear no gun firin'. The back of his head, too, same place he got smashed up in thirty-three.'

Clyde waved his hand in dismissal. 'We got no time to think on Buck now, Bonnie. We've gotta git movin'.'

Bonnie nodded, jumped up off the sofa and danced backwards towards the bedroom. Just short of the door she jerked back, clutching her neck. Blood was spreading across her chest from two small holes.

'Bonnie!' Clyde yelled, sprinting across to her. Bullet holes were opening across her torso, shoulders and head. 'No, Bonnie, ya ain't leavin' me!' He pressed his hands against the blood flow, looking wildly around the room for the shooter. The room was empty, the front door firmly closed.

'Bonnie!' he screamed, tears streaming down his face. He stroked her hair, blood plastering the ends of her dark, sleek bob to her cheeks. 'It's gonna be all right, baby. Yer gonna be jus' fine.' He carried her gently to the sofa, tracing her cupid's bow with his thumb. The light left her eyes, and her body began to fade.

'Moll, ya damn bitch, you doin' this shit?' Clyde roared. 'Bring back my girl, goddamn ya!'

A bullet hole opened on his shoulder. Screaming in pain, he felt the holes silently peppering his chest and neck.

'Show yer face, Moll,' he spluttered, slumping into the space Bonnie's disappearance had left. 'Show yer goddamn face.'

In room 512, Angelique gripped the edges of her swivel chair, breathing heavily. The surveillance screen before her showed no signs of movement; Clyde's body was already fading. Causing a criminal's mode of death to repeat was always tough, especially one who had met a violent end, but the Haitian loa spirits of her ancestors never failed to lend her their strength. She closed her eyes, feeling their energy restoring her own, but an image of Bonnie's dancing form jarred her inner vision. Her guts churned inside her, and she retched as the strains of 'Carmen' sang out from her phone.

'Mama? It's okay,' Angelique choked out. 'You'll have the money later tonight.' She paused to breathe, wishing she had a glass of water. 'But, Mama, I must rest before I raise another. Bonnie, I still feel her inside me, she is fighting to return.' She grimaced as her mother delivered a tirade of abuse before hanging up on her.

'*Merde*,' Angelique whispered, then focused her energy on pushing Bonnie's life force back to the underworld of Guinee to await passage to her ancestors.

The nausea receded, and Angelique sighed with relief. She reached forward, clicking on the mouse to end the live-stream recordings from the bank and room 501. While the files burned to DVD, she wrote on the case in thick black marker: *Bonnie and Clyde (2018)*.

Pausing, she stared at Bonnie's name, then drew a heart around the word. 'Bonnie,' she said out loud, 'I know you loved him, but you deserved a better man than Clyde Barrow.'

Maybe it was because Angelique had raised only male criminals before, but she'd warmed to Bonnie. Smart and sassy, but kind, too; reports from the 1930s had all agreed that it was Clyde and Buck who called the shots, Bonnie often pleading with them to spare their victims.

Angelique stretched and yawned, wishing she could take a nap before the next raising. But Mama had insisted she needed more money before the end of the month to pay her debts, and buy freedom for herself and Angelique's sisters. If she failed to pay up, Mama would find herself in Guinee eyeballing Bonnie, courtesy of a pimp's bullets.

Angelique scanned her DVD collection. One section contained *Goodfellas* (1990), *Bonnie and Clyde* (1992) and *Frank and Jesse* (1994), the original movies. Next to these stood plain cases with *Goodfellas* (2018) and *Frank and Jesse* (2018) written in marker on the spine. She ejected the finished DVD from her laptop, slipped it inside the *Bonnie and Clyde* (2018) case and filed it next to *Goodfellas* (2018).

If only she had time to watch the bank recordings again. For a while she'd thought Buck would blow the whole heist, blundering around yelling, with his rifle cocked like a proud erection. If Bonnie hadn't told him to 'shut it an' git to the car' the three of them would have died at the bank for sure.

Angelique moved to the other end of the shelf, tapping her fingers lightly along a row of thrillers and heist movies. 'Eenie, meenie, miney, moe,' she sang, continuing the rhyme past *The Godfather* (1972) and *The Untouchables* (1987) until her finger landed on *Scarface* (1983).

'Say hello to my little friend,' she rasped, then giggled, a high-pitched, girlish trill, pulling the DVD off the shelf and pressing her lips to Al Pacino's face. She glanced at the monitor for room 501. All clear, not that she'd expected otherwise.

Leaving room 512, she pushed her laden trolley to room 501. Unlocking the door, she guided her cart inside, intercepting the door's swing to close it quietly behind her. All trace of blood and bodies had vanished, but the room required a thorough clean.

Singing 'Rush, Rush' from the *Scarface* soundtrack, she went about her business, vacuuming scattered cigarette ash, replacing towels and sheets, and washing the lipstick-stained mugs. The rifles she stashed beneath the piles of folded linen on her trolley, ready for cleaning and oiling.

When all was in order, Angelique drew a white piece of cardboard and black marker from her apron. She wrote seven words in large, rounded letters and set down the sign on the coffee table. Smiling, she took a single Cohiba Behike cigar from her apron pocket, wrapped with a yellow silk ribbon, placing it beside the sign. Nothing but the best for her guests.

She sat for a moment, gazing at the fat cigar, and then closed her eyes. Her prayers to her psychopomp, loa Ghede Nibo, were quickly answered.

He was here, oh yes. A man who knew how to twist the system, just as she did. His hunger to leave Guinee coursed through her blood, burying itself deep in her marrow. With a sigh, she set him free, then eased her trolley out of the door and back to room 512.

Tired, she sank into her chair, but sat bolt upright when a naked, chubby-faced man materialised on the monitor screen. She gave a childish squeak of excitement as she saw his eyes scan the words on her white sign.

Buongiorno! Your name is Alphonse Gabriel Capone.
The year is 2018.
Love, Moll xxx

Chemicals

Luke West

The flick of a match, the sound of a spark; the wick is lit. I close my eyes and listen as the flicker races down the fuse towards the small chamber filled with combustible chemicals. There's a silence, then a whistle as the little tube flies into the air and explodes in an eruption of glitter-like fragments.

Shortly after, a second firework fills the night sky. Then he leaves. Gone. There's nothing but the sound of gravel crunching underneath his boots as he departs the shed where he's holding me captive. This shed, right here, isn't a place for a girl my age.

I won't see him again until this time tomorrow night. I've done the math: seven nights ago he set off seven fireworks, six nights ago six fireworks, five nights ago five fireworks. A few days later, tonight, there were two. I'm assuming tomorrow night there will be one.

The day after?

I will die.

He's counting me down one explosion of glitter at a time.

I'm lying on my back. The wet grass growing through the rotting floorboards has dampened my shirt. I shiver as a gentle breeze skates across the still lake, through the two missing panels in the shed wall and across my almost-naked skin. I don't mind, though. The chill acts as a gentle scratch at the mosquito bites covering nearly every inch of my body.

My arms and legs stretch out as far as possible in each direction. My ankles and left wrist are bound to stakes. The rope burns my skin as I struggle against its grasp. My right wrist holds onto the stake without risk of injury, a loose rope hanging lazily. I'd cry, but the salt from the tears aggravates the mosquito bites.

I watch the insects hover over my skin, preparing to take another chunk. There's not much free space left, so they start attacking existing wounds. I wiggle as much as I can to scare them off, but they've become immune to my movements.

I'm alone, constantly shaking with fear, in a shed that's hidden amongst the shrubbery where it's almost impossible for anyone to find me, even if someone was stupid enough to wander off the walking track. Exactly what my captor wants.

Through the moonlight, I watch as a lone redback spider cautiously crawls around the wall, determined not to frighten off its next meal. It climbs back into its nest and surveys the stupid insect that has managed to get itself caught. The spider seems to have enough food tonight, a buffet to dine upon. Something I can only dream of. The spider grabs hold of a mosquito and injects it with its venom like it had only seconds to do so.

The night is quiet, a deathly silence that makes the sound of two leaves brushing together seem like a disgruntled clash.

I peek through the missing panels in the wall, my only view of the outside world, and through the shrubbery I see the fairy lights twinkling gently at the carnival on the other side of the lake. From this distance it looks as if the lights dance as one; a continued glow rather than individual flashes.

I'm not sure if it's my imagination, but every now and then I think I can hear the carnies' voices carry across on the wind. I can't make out what they're saying, but it keeps me calm, knowing there are people. I know they aren't close, but they are here, somewhere.

The carnival's grand opening is this Saturday night. Every time Mum and I drove past the lights she would get excited and shake me by the shoulder, cheering. I'd shrug her off, turn up my music and look out my window, pretending that the sight of the rides, food vendors and hungry clown heads with their mouths hanging open didn't get me all excited inside.

Mum wanted to take me, but the idea of being seen with her wasn't my idea of fun. I yelled at her for even having the idea. She was crushed; I could see the hurt in her. I would peep out of the corner of my eye and watch her disappointment. She would quickly shake it off and pretend it didn't hurt her all the way through to her core. I know it did.

The locals have been excited about the grand opening, so much so that the promotional team got behind the event and have been counting down to the opening since forever. Flyers in the letterbox, posters on every street post. It's been a constant subject of conversation within my family.

As I lie on the cold floor, I watch the droplets from last night's storm fall through the cracks in the ceiling and land on the floorboards. My mind begins wandering to the side of my brain that I'm not proud of.

That part of me, the envious part, wants the carnival to fail, to not open on time, for the rollercoaster to drive off its track or something. The thought of all the kids and their disappointed faces ignites the little evil flame inside me.

It's not fair that I'm in this situation. I regret everything I ever said or did to my mum. I know I'm cruel. I've known it all my life. At the end of the day, I deserve how I'm being treated. Being abducted, tied to the ground and left with nothing but the Australian wildlife is karma at its finest.

I can never do anything right, according to my extended family. Mum always attempted to stick up for me, but everybody in the family knew it was her job as a mother, and nobody ever believed a word she said.

I'm probably not a nice person, but I've often wondered if I'm as bad as people make me out to be; they never accept me, never understand my needs. Maybe instead of being punished like this, I should be given sweets and a ride on the pony at the carnival when it opens.

'My mum died last week,' I say out loud, as if speaking the words might heal me faster.

She took her last breath in hospital and it was a huge shock to Dad. He didn't know what to do. He's never had anyone die on him before. Initially it didn't bother me. I couldn't feel a thing. Sure, I had questions. Who would do the chores around the house, like dinner and cleaning? Could I go out on Friday night? Regret quickly dived into the depths of my body.

Her funeral is today. In a few hours her body will be lowered into the ground, covered in dirt, never to be seen again. My heart doesn't just hurt, it *strains*. I think it's actually breaking, physically tearing me apart.

When we found out, Dad thought it would be a good idea for me to take a breather and get some fresh air. I went for a walk, blared some music through my earphones and dissolved the newly found agony much like a painkiller does to a headache. The fresh breeze of the lake made me numb, the excitement of the carnival filled me with shame, and I had to get away. So I wandered off the track, well and truly in the wrong direction.

I stumbled across this shed. It was camouflaged so well that I almost missed it. The wood was rotting and the ceiling looked as if it wouldn't survive the next storm. I went inside. He didn't like my arrival.

Now, as my mum prepares to be lowered into the earth, I'm here wondering whether I'll even get a funeral. Chances are I'll be left here, bound by ropes, rotting in the ground, maybe never to be found again.

I'm left alone in the dark when the carnival lights are turned off. I use the moonlight to survey the wound on my left wrist and then lift my head to check on the wounds around my ankles. They're worse than my wrists; it can't be long until they start dripping with blood. I do my best with my free hand to shoo away the flies, which are eagerly waiting for the good stuff.

The stench of my unwashed body is starting to fill the air. My stomach desperately wants to dry retch as the rotten-garbage smell begins to consume me. For now I can calm it.

It's nighttime and I'm all by myself. It scares the hell out of me. I can hear something slither close by. It's a snake; I know it is. I freaking hate everything about them. My body quivers as it slides nearby. I can almost feel its skin. I'm far too scared to look through the gap in case I come face to face with its bright eyes. Another animal, maybe a possum, runs across the roof.

Out here the animals rule and I'm merely their peasant. *Breathe. Just breathe.*

Somehow I fall asleep. It isn't what you would call beauty sleep, though. My dreams are filled with lies and deception. Dad saying Mum never loved me; him crouched down on the bedroom floor, crying, screaming in pain. In my nightmare, he rightfully blames me for all the wrongs in our family. All our family memories ruined by my need for attention.

Even in my dreams, his heart slowly breaks. I wonder what it might be like to dream of rainbows and lollipops, like the dreams of those who don't have a black cloud stalking them every second of the day.

The sun rises and the winter dew from the lake hovers above the water's surface. I watch the ducks bobbing for fish and listen to the crows screeching their evil good-morning. I don't care about the daytime animals; it's the ones that come out in the dark that frighten me.

I use my right hand, the one that remains unrestrained, to reach into my bag and search blindly for breakfast. Today he has left me an egg. Not boiled, not scrambled, just an egg. When your body hits a certain hunger level you don't care about delicacies, you simply bite into the object and force it down your throat as quickly as possible. It's certainly not nice, but it keeps the gurgling complaints from my stomach mute for a few hours.

After breakfast, I allow a morning tear to slide down my left cheek. I'm never going to see my mum again. Even though I treated her like absolute crap, there was always love behind the anger; I just never told her. She always tried to be there for me, was always more than willing to drop everything to dry the tears. If ever I had problems at school, or just felt a bad mood wash over me, she was there.

I never thanked her or showed any sign of appreciation. I can't even remember the last time I told her I loved her.

I spend most of the afternoon squinting to watch the carnies across the lake. From here they are like bees, buzzing around on their daily duties. The Ferris wheel is up and looking magnificent. The swinging chairs are ready to spin, but the carnies appear to be having issues with the ghost train. I like to imagine one of them absolutely losing it over a technical glitch. It's more fun that way. They sound far too happy for my liking.

It's dark again now, my sixth night here. I can't work out whether the shiver my body is experiencing is from the cold or the fear about my captor turning up at any minute.

I inhale and exhale with as much strength as I can muster. I try to focus on the air rushing down my windpipe and into the heart of my anxiety, each breath extinguishing the fire.

I can do this. I have to get out of this place.

Like clockwork, the crunching gravel beneath his boots breaks the silence. He's still a short distance away. I pull the ropes as hard as I can and struggle against their grasp, as always. Maybe my fear will encourage more strength. I can jump him when he opens the door, make a run for it and get to the carnival where people can help me. He's bigger than me, but maybe the shock will add to my strength.

Nope, not today. The ropes won't budge, and I have barely any fight left in me.

He's closer now, and if I ever happen to make it back to my own bed that crunching sound of gravel will haunt my dreams forever.

The husky intake of his breath sounds blocked by a lifetime of cigarettes and the more-than-occasional scotch on the rocks. He stands at the door and unbolts the lock. He circles me, not once removing his eyes from mine. I'm too scared to blink in case it annoys him.

He tiptoes behind me, and no matter how much I try to turn my head I can't see him. *Please don't hurt me,* I repeat in my head over and over. *Just give me a break.*

Suddenly his hands grip my wrists violently and I use that internal anxiety to muster the loudest scream I possibly can. He's frustrated that I've managed to loosen the constraints, pissed I've broken his routine. He tightens the ropes with all his might, almost cutting off my circulation. There's no way I'll ever escape.

He grunts in annoyance and throws tomorrow's egg in my bag with force. He stops. Takes a deep breath and quickly gathers himself back to a calm state, one breath at a time. His rough hands gently touch my skin, quickly finding their way to my boobs. I quiver and he laughs.

"Sshh,' he whispers as he strokes my hair.

He uses his fingertips to crawl gently up my arm, one finger at a time. He stops at my neck and tickles. He laughs a little.

I focus on the spider in its nest and pray it will choose me as its next meal. 'Why are you doing this?' I whisper through tears. 'How could you do this to someone?'

He doesn't answer. He stands up, tiptoes back around my body and faces me again. He smiles and then leaves, slamming the door behind him. He fiddles with the lock until it's secure. Then he prepares for his nightly firework show.

I turn my head and squint through the gap, doing my best to watch, just like I'm supposed to. 'Why don't you talk to me?' I scream with confidence. 'We could be friends. Yes, let's be friends.' I'm desperate; I'll do anything.

Instead, I hear the familiar flick of a match and soon enough the pretty fireball screams into the air before it blasts into a million little pieces. I wait eagerly for another firework. Maybe my theory is wrong. Maybe he's just going to keep me here forever. Maybe we'll be friends.

No. It's not my day. He leaves and I'm left alone.

The only cheers come from the carnies across the lake. If only the bastards knew what that firework meant. If only the sick bastards actually investigated why a firework is screaming into the sky from the middle of nowhere. I should be so lucky.

I look through the gap in the wall and up at the stars. I cry again, and allow my bladder to empty itself into my already soaked pants. I squint and stare up at the sky, trying to take my mind someplace else. I'm thankful for its art tonight. It really has put on a pretty display for my last night of breathing.

Imagine living a life with a full understanding of when you're going to die. You know the exact hour, the exact minute, and the exact second. Some people might prefer knowing how many days they have left, but what if their time was sooner than they anticipated? What if you were told you only had days, hours and minutes until you departed Earth?

What would you do?

Would you carry out a bank robbery and blow all the cash? Go dance in the Moulin Rouge?

Perhaps you'd want to know what it's like to hold a gun to someone's head. Stab someone through the chest to feel it penetrate the skin.

Perhaps you'd want to do something nice and help an elderly woman cross the road. But then you might want to know the feeling of pushing her in front of a truck.

I've always known that at some point I'm going to die; I just didn't expect it to be tomorrow. I guess it's one of those things we keep in the back of our minds and don't often think about. I mean, at the end of the day, who's going to think about their impending death right before they go to sleep?

Me.

How could I not? Time is running out.

I wake up the next morning with the familiar realisation: today is the day my story will end. I'm worried that I didn't have enough appreciation of the sun rising. Should I have thought of another childhood memory and relived it in my mind, changing the part where I often yelled at Mum, replacing it with something more loving?

The day drags on, and for once I'm okay with that. I watch the sun travel its path into the afternoon and wonder if time will pass even slower if I stare at it. It does place the day in slow motion, but what's the point of waiting? All good things have to come to an end, right?

You can fill a cold bath in the heart of summer and get in it, but soon enough you have to pull out the plug and feel the heat again. All you're left with is droplets of water. Scattered memories gradually grow smaller and smaller, and life, like that bath-water life, eventually dries up.

I think about the funeral. Mum will be in the ground by now. Strangely, I've never felt closer to her. Dad will be a wreck, comforted by his family, who will be complaining about my lack of attendance behind his back. 'Another stunt,' they'll say, 'and at her own mum's funeral.'

The sad thing is, nobody will come looking. The normality of my situation is my own karma.

The egg from yesterday has digested to the point where I should visit a toilet. Even though nobody's here, there's nothing more embarrassing than shitting your pants. I'm wearing a nice skirt, too.

Nighttime falls and panic well and truly kicks in. What's it going to feel like to die? How will he do it? Will it hurt? I'm never going to be a part of this world again, and I'm not okay with that.

The ducks stop diving for fish and the birds hide from their nighttime predators. I can't hide, though. I can't even fend for myself. Death is something I have to face. He'll be here any minute now.

The air is quiet. The gravel underneath his boots crunches louder tonight, like he's a little excited. I let a tear run down my face. I pray it slides down my cheek and vanishes before he sees it. I want to die with my head held high.

He unlocks the door and stands there. He slowly unbuttons his jacket and showcases his portfolio of cutlery. A creepy smile now presents across his face. I cry, not caring now about remaining strong. I'm shaking with fear; I hope that maybe, just maybe, he'll show a little heart.

With one step at a time, he slowly walks behind me.

'Please, just please,' I whisper, with every last bit of courage I have in me.

He laughs loudly. 'You aren't escaping me that easily.'

Knowing that I won't win this battle, I begin praying for it to be over. *I will get out of this darkness. I will escape this nightmare.*

Without any further warning, from behind me he lifts the knife over my head, just above my chest, and stabs me right through the heart. I scream in pain. It's the most excruciating thing I have ever experienced. I scream loudly and pray for someone, anyone, to hear my cry.

I sit up, grasping for air. My face is sweaty and my cheeks are flushed. The bath water is colder than before. I search all around me, waiting for him to jump out of the darkness again, to finish me off once and for all. He's gone, nowhere to be seen. How could he leave me in this state? On the floor, I notice scattered pills. I must have knocked them over.

'Darling, are you okay in there?' Mum whispers through the closed door, her voice filled with the usual morning happiness that, when in my darkest of minds, is the reason I want her dead. She's the bubble of joy in our family. Like glue, she keeps everyone together.

'No,' I whisper back, not loudly enough for her to hear.

My eyes remain focused on a single pill. It's crazy that a tiny little pebble of crushed powder has the ability to keep the travelling carnival from moving towns. The psychologist said, 'Seven days on these and you'll start to notice the difference in your mood. You'll be happier.' I thought of nothing but my inner carnival. I had hope.

You see, when you mix hydrogen and oxygen together you can cause an explosion. I guess that's what happened in my mind at some point in my life: a mini explosion. Except that the chemical imbalance in my mind is serotonin, responsible for carrying signals along and between the nerves. Without it, mental illness thrives. A Disneyland for depression, and I had a season pass to the black dog.

'Darling?' Mum whispers again, this time with a little more concern.

'Yes, yes, Mum, I'm fine,' I say with aggravation.

I listen to her footsteps walking back down the hallway and lay my head on the bath ledge. I close my eyes and picture my carnival. The crowds flow through the gates with excitement while a display of brightly coloured fireworks bursts above them. Various shades of pink, yellow, blue and green take over the night sky.

I see my mum there. She's waving at me through the gates, begging me to come in. She laughs with Dad, who's just inside the entrance, unsure of his surroundings. Although nobody inside the grounds knows each other, they all have one thing in common: they are happy.

I look through the fence at the people riding the rollercoaster. Although fearful of what might happen around the corner, they are all enjoying themselves. The lines are so long they know they'll only get one ride. They go upside down and around the loops. Some scream, some cry; they all handle it differently. They laugh when the cart lifts them high into the sky, and scream when it throws them back down again. They don't want it to ever stop.

One day it will stop.

I can't wait to enter this land of happiness. I haven't been to the carnival since I was a child, back when I didn't appreciate it enough. Now I'd do anything for the attendant to let me in the gate again.

Seven nights ago, when I took those pills, there were seven fireworks counting down until my carnival opened.

Six nights ago there were six fireworks.

Five nights ago there were five fireworks.

A few days later, tonight, there are none. The carnival is open, but I'm just not ready to enter yet.

Date Night

Tania Cossich

Candle shadows dance around glass bowls as the light of Valentine's Day shifts into the night. Red rose petals spill down the lengths of white tables that lie between the windows and bar of the old pub, spaces that wait to host introductions for hopefuls.

Danni had spent longer than needed to step out her front door. She had tossed her clothes from her wardrobe in despair before she had managed to wriggle into a low-cut black dress. After applying a touch of lipstick, a brush of black on lashes, and a feeble smile to herself in the mirror, she had set off on her quest to find her 'special one'.

Love is a delicate kiss traced on a drowsy forehead. Danni had never fully understood this; she preferred to elbow her partner awake and tell him to clean the sleep from his eyes. Yet she always held a soft spot for the weary-hearted.

Although lines burrow deeper into Danni's face with each passing year, she is not unattractive. Men are strangely drawn to her, like sleepwalkers to the edge of a cliff. Even the dullest of men sense an unknown in her.

Murmured greetings bubble between arrivals to the special event. Danni joins the group of preened women on their best behaviour who seem to hover near the tables. The competition is tough: a shapely blonde, a bouncy brunette, a smiling Scandinavian, and several other women primed for their dream to emerge from the shadows. The scant selection of potential males eyes their preferred type from behind pints of beer.

Kevin enters the bar late. He instantly attracts with his man-of-mystery appeal and clean-cut confidence, all contained in a buff body. Longing ladies circle around him, and Danni can almost hear their silent screams: *Pick me. Pick me.* She leaves the waves of rising oestrogen to cool off at the bar.

Group dynamics make her head hurt. She has been good so far, but knows her social graces could rapidly decline. She had started with a non-alcoholic drink, ensuring she didn't spit on anyone too early in the night. It's a bad habit she fails to notice until the listener has wiped their face a few times more than usual and retreated from the conversation. With the main male attraction surrounded by a posse of shining prospects, she seeks refuge in more serious, liquid sustenance.

She digs in her bag to pay for her espresso martini. Three coffee beans relax on the frothy surface. *Whatever you do, don't chew on the beans,* she reminds herself. Her mouth seems to consider the spaces between her bright white teeth and her gums the best place to store dark bits of food for consumption at some later time. In the wild, it might have worked as a midnight snack, but here it will only serve to widen the gap between Danni and the love challengers.

She had noticed Kevin's empty glass when she sidled past him towards the bar. Knowing he'd soon be thirsty, she stays near the bar to talk to Sonia, who has peeled off from the unsuitably young males; the organiser should have done better.

Danni is similarly affronted by the age gap on offer. Age is not the main issue for Danni, but she continues to speak to Sonia. She hopes that Sonia's esoteric dress sense and stark difference from Danni's own style might work to her advantage, although it could go either way since Danni is no judge of men's tastes.

Sonia's sentences begin to reel in on themselves, and with each gulp of cocktail her head droops closer to her glass, leaving her cleavage, signposted by an amethyst cross on a chain, to do the talking.

Kevin walks behind Danni to refill with the local specialty on tap: a pot of cold Victoria Bitter. The pub has filled with bodies that push a fellow thirsty bloke to Kevin's left. With Sonia angled on his right, Danni, who knows her charms aren't enough to trap Kevin, glides into a position designed to limit his escape options as he exchanges notes for coins with the bartender. The noose closed, Kevin will need to dodge the gauntlet of her building desire.

Kevin is easy pickings, she thinks, but when he turns, he is the one to begin a conversation. Danni feels the balance shift. A warning pumps through her mind. She prefers to be the scientist and not the specimen in social contexts. Intimacy is a spider that loops inside Danni's chest, waiting for a false move to strike poison through her hopes. She uses her martini to calm herself, to keep verbal gaffs in place as the fluid busies her tongue.

From its wide-rimmed glass, the martini slushes past her pursed lips and runs into the crease of her chin. No problem, she thinks, surely it's hardly noticeable. *Keep it cute and make it work for you.*

She wipes her lips slowly with her fingertips in a replica of late-night television advertisements featuring underdressed young women. Danni notices that Kevin is unable to take his eyes off her actions.

As she basks in his testosterone-driven attention, she tries to quell the sense that threatens to drown her like a tsunami. It is the idea that Kevin has stayed to talk to her, with her sagging pheromones, and the cleavage-speaking Sonia out of simple politeness, and respite from the overwhelming desires of the younger women.

Danni's need to be desired kicks back at the thought; it is her he wants. She knows it; he knows it. As she slow-time wipes the espresso from her mouth, pulling her lower lip down and open, she knows she has his full attention. This time she arches her fingers to her top lip to repeat the gesture, plans a longer stroke, chin out, slightly up, a slow blink of the eyes, deep breaths that raise her assets.

She doesn't get any further than laying her finger on her top lip. Softer and wetter than it should be, Danni pulls her finger into focus and notices what Kevin has been observing in stunned silence. A great espresso martini moustache has gatecrashed her fantasies.

She tilts her head down to wipe off the rest of the espresso martini with the back of her hand. When she looks up again, not only has the brown alcoholic drink spilt down her white top, as though she has lactated, but her booby helper, Sonia, has resurfaced long enough to suggest that Danni wipes away the lipstick she's managed to smudge across her face. Sonia whispers it to her conspiratorially, as only a drunk person can: loudly.

Kevin smirks into his beer as he tilts his glass back. So easy for some people, Danni thinks. She tries to recover a semblance of esteem. Starts small; plans to work up to bigger stuff.

'So, what do you do?' Glib. Half wishes she had started with bigger questions first.

He perfect-teeth smiles. 'Dealer.'

'Oh. Cars, cards or hotels?' Go, super-clever Danni. Nice.

'Drugs.'

A beat.

'Oh. That's nice.' Determined not to lose her composure again. 'Done it long?' She is past being picky; a dealer will do nicely, thanks.

He shrugs, a fullstop planted firmly into the conversation. She looks into his lovely green eyes, knowing they alone would be enough for her to forgive any indiscretions.

'What do you do?' It should have been his question, but it comes from Sonia's cleavage.

'I'm a dispatcher,' Danni retorts.

Kevin pays back. 'Oh yeah? Buses, trucks, packages?'

'Humans.'

'Oh.'

Take that, she thinks. I may be your perfect match yet.

The air-conditioner kicks into gear. Danni feels the icy breeze, sees it force Kevin's shirt against his broad shoulders, and the hair on his forearms stands to attention as nubs race up his skin. She thinks of her dinner the previous night. Tender. Young; easy to carve.

Kevin shivers and mumbles that he needs to relieve himself.

Sonia's drunkenness swings into and away from Danni's face with a, 'He's nice.'

Danni watches Kevin leave and decides to head home. As she announces her impending exit, Sonia slurs a question.

'Can you give me a lift home?'

Sonia is far from Danni's type, but with Kevin gone and the rest of the pack a background gaggle, Danni looks at this woman and knows she would be disappointed to have sharpened her tools for no reason.

Joe Vale's Last Case

Charmaine Clancy

It was three minutes past two am and I was kissing the pavement outside a bar whose name I couldn't remember after searching for a dame I wish to god I *didn't* remember — just another typical Saturday night. I pushed my palms into the asphalt, ignoring the tiny shards of glass biting into them. Before I could rise, the second blast thrust me back to the ground. Flames spat and cursed from open windows. All right, that was new.

I got to my feet, staggered a few steps and spat out a mouthful of gravel. Pulsating sirens. The crunch of running feet. Great, the cops were here already. Police cars blocked the alley exit like a brick wall. I turned the other way. An actual brick wall. Huh.

Assessing a potential crack between two officers, I readied myself to gallop. Old instincts, I guess. I had no reason to run ... this time.

A young cop, still as green as beer on St Patrick's Day, stared wide-eyed like a trout flapping on deck, into the blaze. 'Were you in there, mister? Holy smoke!'

I'd inhaled a lot of that smoke, and no, Father Fitzpatrick had not blessed it.

'Is anyone still inside?'

The cops' Ford Mercurys parted, triggering the hope I get watching a roulette wheel spin. *Tat-tat-tat-tat-tat. Kerplunk.* Always lands on odds when I've placed my chips on evens.

A cherry-red fire engine blocked the exit greedily as it screeched in close. Young men jumped about, connected hoses and patted backs. If they could beat fire with camaraderie, it was a goner.

'There could be people inside, we have to move quickly.' The rookie cop flailed his arms about.

I could've told him it was too late for that. The people left inside would be coming out feet first. I suppose I could also have told him they'd been dead since before the flaming cocktail took hold, but I figured it was best not to mess with stuff that was none of my business. Police investigations should *definitely* be none of my damn business.

I swiped dirt off my jacket, now soggy from the damp gutter, and stepped back, just far enough to give me access to the alley's exit. Hanging around would only mean trouble, and it should be obvious by now that I was pretty good at finding my own trouble.

Okay, it was obvious to me. You'll understand when we get there.

'Hey, you.' Damn, it was the rookie. 'Stop, you can't leave. Who are you, anyway?'

My fist unclenched, and with a tired grin I reached for the wallet in my pocket, pulled it out and flicked it open.

The rookie squinted at my licence. 'Oh, Mr Vale. Wow. I've heard about you.'

'Really?' That was all I needed.

'Yeah, the boys down at the station are always telling stories about your cases. Heard you took down half of Valceni's organisation. You were a really big player back in the day.'

My chest puffed out.

His eyes travelled up and down my worn suit. 'What happened?'

My chest deflated.

'Vacation,' I grumbled.

The rookie flicked a thumb toward the burning building. 'You working a case, sir?'

Sir. I was starting to like this kid. 'Yeah, sure, a case. That's me, PI for hire, good ol' Detective Joe Vale. Dead end this time.' I glanced down at the PI licence before shoving it back in my pocket.

'I might have to talk to you about this later, sir. Are you still at Swanston Street?'

An alarm went off. I leaned over him with my full doorway-filling size and growled, 'You don't know me and I don't know you, so how come you're all of a sudden familiar with my office premises?'

He shrugged. 'The address is on your licence.'

I pulled my wallet back out and flipped it open. 'So it is. Well, look at that. Right there with my PI number, FU6339. You get that, too?'

'Sure did, sir. Well, someone will probably give you a call tomorrow.'

'I'll be sitting by the phone like an ugly dame waiting for a date.' I grinned and waved to the dope as I left.

The sun burned the sidewalk, casting busy shadows as mugs made their way to work. I swallowed again in a useless attempt to moisten my throat. It was drier than dust and my eyelids ached in their struggle against gravity. I hadn't slept but for ten minutes, and that had been in the back of my car.

A brass band had taken over my head and was performing all the latest toe-tapping hits. Damn, I hate swing music. Right now, I'd kill an orphan and kiss his dead mother for a couple of aspirin.

I'd hit a dead-end last night. My last lead to find the girl ended in gunshots and burning buildings. Today, the coroner would be identifying a charcoal crisp as John Doe, and news would leak that gumshoe Joe Vale was the only survivor.

Valceni's guys might not be the smartest kids in class, but they'd eventually put two and two together and come up with four. As in, four grand laid out to a certain Mike the Mouse to track down the piece of fluff who turned against Valceni and was lined up to rat him out in his upcoming trial. If I didn't find the girl soon, they'd have someone else find her.

I was unshaven, my suit was rumpled, and my pores seeped last night's bourbon. Still, I had an idea, and that was worth something.

There was bound to be something on the girl back at the office that could strike up a fresh lead. I just had to get hold of the Valceni case files.

I took the stairs to the second floor of the tired little complex in busy Carlton. Taking the stairs was an old habit; it was easier to get away if things turned sour. But it was also because the dusty metal lift with the door that wouldn't close all the way looked like it could get you killed as effectively as a slug to the chest.

I could just make out the outline of the words JOE VALE PI on the frosted glass; some monkey had scraped off the lettering. Probably the same monkey who'd stuck the eviction notice on the door. I ripped it off and crumpled it in one hand with the expertise that only comes with practice.

I crossed the musty office and opened the blinds, just enough to see, not enough to challenge my pounding head. Through the slits of light, I could see two things of interest: to my right a filing cabinet with the bottom drawer pulled open, and to my left, a half empty bottle of whiskey on the desk next to a dirty glass. The indecision actually paralysed me for a moment.

I pulled the file on Valceni and the one on O'Shea, tipped back another glass of the whiskey and headed to the desk for a refill.

The file told a story. Valceni's dealings were growing, and he now had a stronghold on the streets of Melbourne. A short war had broken out between the Italian gangsters and Melbourne's original mob, the Irish boys, headed up by Martin O'Shea. The Irish were being pushed out, and O'Shea saw an opportunity to hang onto his connections here, rather than lose it all. He broke bread with Valceni and became the Italian's dancing monkey, his link between the boys on the street and the big dealers.

Everything was going smoothly until O'Shea's daughter got involved with the wrong kinda boy: the nice kind. A young lad from a family of judges, the sort with a reputation so clean it sparkled. Neither family broke out the cigars, so the two lovesick kids eloped to Sydney. The honeymoon was cut short on account of the groom suffering from a chest infection, the kind caused by a couple of slugs. Maggie was dragged home.

I picked up a newspaper clipping taken from *The Argus* social columns. It was an announcement for the engagement of Maggie O'Shea and Vincent Valceni Jnr. Dated just two weeks after Maggie's first husband was shot dead. A picture in grey tones accompanied the announcement. There she was, wild untameable locks that just had to be red, big sad eyes framed with determination, and full lips curled into a tiger's smile.

The following Saturday night there'd been a big engagement party. Scribbled notes in the file said she'd kissed and greeted every guest warmly before taking the opportunity to sneak out to the valet, steal a shiny new Chrysler and slip away into the night.

Maggie O'Shea was now officially a most wanted. The Victorian Police Department had this girl tagged as a Royal Commission witness, Valceni wanted her silenced, and the old Irish man claimed he just wanted his daughter home safe and sound.

It was all there in the files, even notes on Maggie's call to the office two days ago. Yep, everything except a way to find her.

I couldn't give up. Wouldn't. I was *that* guy, the one you go to when you need to get the job done, when you need to find your man, or dame. I was him. Never failed a case and I wouldn't start now. I had to find Maggie before they did. If only my mind wasn't so darn beat up.

I poured another glass with conviction and stared a little longer at the picture of Maggie. I heard the door open, but didn't care enough to react. Instead, I tossed back the rest of the glass, refilled it and slid it across the table. 'One glass, have to share.'

She was short, blonde and the perkiest gal I'd ever seen. Her curves had so much pointing at me I almost didn't notice the sweet little Derringer in her shaking hand.

'Where is she?' she half spat, half cried the words.

'No drink, then?' I shrugged and tipped it down my throat, never one to let really bad drink go to waste.

'You know where she is, you'll tell me, or I'll—'

'Put the toy away, sweets, you've got enough firepower naturally, you don't need that.'

She frowned, crinkled her pretty little forehead and then beamed all smiles as she dropped the .22 Special into her pocketbook. No transaction. Just like that, from serious and sad to giggles and grins. That there should have tipped me off.

'Yes, yes, you'll tell me, won't you?' She leaned over as she spoke. Oh baby, those were nice round— 'I know she contacted you, Mr Shade, and I'm going crazy out of my mind with worry.' Her head bowed slightly. False modesty. I've met shy girls, and they weren't built like this.

'Sit down and rest your pins, sweets. Tell me who it is you're looking for and why you think I can help.' I waved to the chair opposite.

Ha! She knew her commodity. She dragged the chair around to the side of the desk so she could sit close to me. Close enough to touch, to just reach across and —

'Maggie O'Shea. And you're a dick for hire.'

'So I am, but why don't we start with your name?'

'Lizzie.'

'Lizzie,' I repeated. She was as much a Lizzie as this bootleg was cognac. 'Truth is, sweets, I don't know where Miss O'Shea is. If I did, what makes you think I'd tell you?'

She gasped and thrust a palm against her breast. I didn't know if it was to fake indignation or to point out her curves. She really didn't need a billboard to sell that product. 'Maggie's in terrible danger, and I told you, I'm just —'

'Yeah, yeah, going crazy with worry. Short trip, I'd say.'

'Why, you ...' Curled lips, bared teeth; her hand formed a perfect claw, ready to tear me to shreds. Then a flick was switched and she became Miss Demure again. Almost daring me, she said, 'You don't know nothing.'

'I know plenty, maybe not who done it, or why they done it, or even who they done it to, but you just try me on whiskey names, which horse to back in the fourth, or how to turn out a fluffy omelette. Yeah, you just try me.'

'Stop fooling, Mr Vale. I must find my sister.'

Sister. I was tight, but I wasn't that tight. This dame was no more Maggie's sister than I was. She obviously didn't have any clue about the O'Shea girl's whereabouts or she wouldn't be here. As far as I could see, there was no sensible reason to keep this loon with me.

She read my face like the morning news and her breasts heaved defeat.

I let the shower run cold. It was hotter than a roast dinner outside and I needed to sober up some. There was something in those files, something I'd missed when looking through the bottle.

When I emerged from the bathroom, a towel draped my hips. It was still dry and I was soaked. My head hurt right through to my toes, and the thought of rubbing my hair dry was about as appealing as kissing a rattlesnake.

'You're dripping water on the carpet.' The scratchiness in her voice made me wonder why I'd brought her along. She sat up in bed, letting the covers fall to her waist, and then I remembered.

'It's not your carpet, so why worry, sweets?' We were in a cheap motel on the wrong side of a town that didn't have a right side. My place was too hot after last night, and this dame was fishier than an aquarium so I didn't want to risk whatever might be waiting for us back at hers.

I snatched up the file from the nightstand, lost the towel and fell back onto the bed. Lizzie placed a hand on my shoulder. Normally that would've been enough to make me forget the case altogether, but there in the open file was her picture. Those eyes, begging the camera— begging *me*—to help her.

That's when I saw it. I flicked back to the article covering Maggie's disappearance from her own engagement party, then the guest list, and finally the stolen car report. 'Get dressed, sweets, we caught a lead.'

Lizzie squealed and hugged me tight. 'You're amazing, Joe. Do you know where Maggie is?'

'No, but I have a lead and we have to strike while it's hot.'

'Then what are you doing now?' She raised a sketched brow.

'Okay, we can still strike while the lead is slightly warm.' And I pulled the covers over us.

'Where are we?'

Had her voice grated on me right from the start? To my horror, I was sobering up. 'This, sweets, is the studio of one Karl Zeager, photographer to the rich and famous.'

'Who?'

If you've ever heard a toddler play an untuned violin with a cat, you would've found her tone familiar. I made a mental note to lose this ditzy dame first chance I got.

'This Karl whatsie-ger, he's got Maggie?'

Forget the mental note, I'd have it tattooed on my chest.

I looked once again into those haunting eyes of the girl in the photo. *Help me, Joe*, they seemed to plead. No, not me, not Joe Vale. She was pleading with the photographer. Zeager.

Getting Lizzie to wait in the car was like asking a rabid dog to sit and stay. She argued, whined and cursed until I subdued her with a promise to return in a dash and kissed her lips. It was also a good way to silence that godawful voice.

When I returned, she was curled up in her seat, snoozing like a puppy. I tried to slip in behind the wheel without waking her. She was more attractive like this—unconscious.

It was almost an hour's drive, and she slept and drooled all the way. By the time we'd arrived in Mont Albert Lane, I'd convinced myself the crazy dame and I might actually be able to make a go of it. Maybe I'd even get out of the business, find a chump job. I'd just have to finish this one last case. Get to the girl before the mob's goons found her. I couldn't let them have her. I'd never had a failure before and I wasn't going to let this, my last case, be my first.

I'd show Valceni. I'd show him.

Lizzie sat up, wiped the back of her hand across her mouth and stretched her arms out in a yawn, highlighting all her best features. Beyond the row of Baldwyn homes—some sandstone, some stucco, but all with with grand gates—the sun sank in a blaze of pink and orange.

'We there?'

'Yeah, sweets, time to act.'

Her eyes bulged. 'I can't go up, she won't let us in if she sees me.'

I leaned back in my seat and crossed my arms. 'Her own sister?'

Lizzie inspected her razor-sharp nails with great interest. 'It's, um, complicated. She's so scared of Papa, she might not trust me.'

She was lying. I liked her a little more for that.

'All right, sweets, we'll play it your way. You wait in the car, I'll go see Maggie.' I flipped open the file and pulled out the clipping.

Now her bottom lip stuck out. 'I don't like the way you keep ogling Maggie's picture. You love her more than me.' She flopped back and crossed her arms.

'Now, sweets,' I crooned, 'this picture's okay, she's a looker, I'm not going to lie to you. But you know what I like ogling.'

She grinned, uncrossed her arms and arched her back. I could almost have ignored that twang, the melody of cats fighting in the moonlight, to get treated to this view every day. Almost.

I rang the buzzer at the double wooden doors, ready with my spiel.

'Hello?' Honey-smooth.

'Joe Vale, PI,' I said. 'We need to talk, Miss O'Shea.'

The silence ticked away. The trick was in the waiting, without appearing to be waiting.

'How do I kno—'

'We spoke on the phone, only a few days ago, Miss O'Shea. Now, I don't want to alarm you, but there are some very bad men looking for you, Miss O'Shea, and your friend, Mr Zeager, really can't keep you safe.'

'You know Karl?' Even when afraid and suspicious, her voice was singing angels.

'We spoke earlier today, he sent me to you.'

'I'll call him.'

'Mr Zeager agreed that he would head out of town immediately. Your father made the connection, Miss O'Shea. He realised that Zeager had to be the one helping you. Your friend can't risk leading them to you, or even taking a call from you. Do you understand?'

Tick. Tick. Tick.

Tick. Tick.

'Come on in, Mr Vale.' The sweetest invitation.

She pulled open the door and there she was, long and elegant, a turquoise-silk concoction draped about her in the way uptown girls were wearing gowns this year. Her long red waves were pushed back with a band, showing off those big sad eyes. If class had looked like this when I was a boy, I might've paid more attention to my teacher.

'Is there anyone else here, Miss O'Shea? Someone who can help me protect you, or staff to keep an eye out.'

She turned to me. 'My name is not O'Shea, it's Clarkson. Clarkson was my husband's name and now it is my name, even if my father won't accept it. That is something you would know if you really were Joe Vale.'

I smiled and reached in my coat for my .45 automatic, but froze when I saw the snub-nose .38 in her hand. It wasn't a toy like Lizzie's. It was a nickel-plated Smith and Wesson, and it would definitely do the job.

'So that must've been Mr Vale's body found in the nightclub fire. It's all over the papers. Tell me, who are you really?' Her words didn't tremble even once. She was accusing me and yet her voice carried the tone of lovers whispering in the dark.

'I'm —'

'Not alone,' a parakeet squawked as a Derringer was pointed straight into Maggie O'Shea's back.

'Lizzie,' Maggie murmured, dropping her gun to the floor and raising her hands.

'Wait.' To say I was confused would be saying ducks quack. 'You two really are sisters?' I was strangely disappointed that Lizzie was on the level.

'Is that what she told you? Oh, Lizzie, why have you come here?'

'You know why, Maggie. We can run now. We just get rid of the lug and no one else will know about us.' Lizzie let out a crazed chortle.

'Zeager's already taken care of, so how about you tell me what's going on here, sweets?' I kept my hand resting on the handle of my pistol.

'Karl? No.' Maggie's shoulders sagged.

I shrugged. 'If it makes you feel any better, it took a lot of work to get him to spill the beans on your location. He didn't buy my Detective Vale line either.'

'What do you care?' We both jumped when Lizzie shouted, 'A photographer now? How could you Maggie, first that stupid college boy and now this.'

Maggie turned to face Lizzie. 'No, sweetie, no, Karl was a friend, that's all. A good friend. He knew me before I met Roger, back when you and I ... Karl understood.'

'Wait, you're not sisters, are you?'

'And you're not a detective,' Lizzie snarled, 'so you must be one of Valceni's goons. You didn't come to help Maggie, you came to kill her.'

'Well, didn't *you*?' I counted.

'Maybe. I haven't decided yet.'

'Lizzie,' Maggie crooned, 'you have to let me go.'

'Why? So you can find another man? You loved me. I know you did.'

'Lizzie, we were kids. I didn't know what I wanted. Then I met Roger.'

Spittle bubbled on Lizzie's tight mouth. 'Then I'm glad I told your father where you two eloped to. Got him dead, good and proper.' She laughed again, a high-pitched cackle. 'Love him so much? Then you can join him.' She raised her gun toward Maggie's temple. Before she could pull the trigger, she was thrown across the floor.

She lay in the pooling blood, gazing up at me, looking … offended. 'But you … why?'

'Sorry, sweets, can't let you do that.' After all, I had integrity.

'You fell in love with her through a photograph, a stupid photograph in the paper. Even in black and white, you could see something … special in her.' A small trickle of blood escaped her lips. 'What about me? I've got something special.'

'Two of them,' I agreed.

I stepped toward Maggie. I've got smarts. Not book smarts, but street smarts. I always knew how to think quick and make the most of an opportunity, like the way I did when I killed Joe Vale and the others in the bar. But one type of smarts I've never had is with women. Just your average dope when it comes to them. Seemed inevitable that one would eventually be my downfall.

As I moved toward Maggie O'Shea, I was thinking how lovely she looked in the dimming light, how nice it would be to touch that wave of red hair, but also, how I'd miss that crazy dame, Lizzie. Not the voice, of course, but her curves, the way they moulded themselves into my hands … I even had a moment to think back to my first gal, the one who'd got me sent up river for a while after I offed her husband.

So I wasn't at all surprised to find that when I stood up close to Maggie O'Shea, close enough to feel her breath on my lips, my heart burned through my chest.

My Colt clattered on the tiles next to her revolver. She gasped. I fell to my knees. She knelt down in front of me and placed a slender hand on my chest. It came away covered in blood. We both turned to Lizzie, but her eyes were now wide and focused somewhere beyond this world.

'You're shot,' Maggie cried. 'You saved my life and now you're shot.'

'I …' I could've told her I was a bad guy, the baddest. Instead, I collapsed onto my back.

She leaned over me, her hair draping across my forehead. I reached up and pressed my hand to her cheek. Her skin was warm under my touch, hot even. Or maybe my hands were cold. I'd seen enough chumps fade out to know this was only one step from the end.

I wasn't finished. I couldn't go like this. I tried to tell her. The words gurgled and spluttered into nothing.

'Shh.' Tears, actual tears fell from her face and landed on mine. I wished I could feel them. 'I don't know your name. I don't care who you were. You did the right thing in the end, I want you to know that. Your last act was a good one. Maybe that'll make up for some things. Who can tell?' Her lips brushed my forehead, then kissed my cheeks and finally paused on my lips.

It was over. I felt so cold as my heat, my life, pumped out of the hole in my chest. Lizzie's toy. Turned out to be enough to do the job.

I was going to die, and what was worse, I was going to die a nice guy. My hands slipped from Maggie's cheeks to her throat. I wondered if I had enough strength to finish the job.

I didn't.

Joe Vale returned to his office on Monday to find the door unlocked and an eviction notice in the wastepaper bin. Someone had also helped themselves to his gin.

It took only a moment for him to notice that the files on Valceni and Mrs Clarkson were gone, but he knew that Jimmy would have them. The guy was a lug, but he was close enough in stature to pass for Joe, as long as no one looked too closely.

The meeting with Mr O'Shea's goon was too important to miss. Mrs Clarkson was no threat to Valceni or O'Shea; she just wanted to start fresh. Joe knew it had been risky, but Jimmy was a pretty good negotiator, and it wouldn't do to have your client find out you couldn't make the meeting because you had to spend seven days as a guest in the big house for unpaid fines.

Joe sat down at his desk. Jimmy would be calling in any minute to let him know how the meeting went. In the meantime, there was still a shot or two left in the bottle.

Life's Not Perfect

Liane McDermott

Post: *So proud of these girls ... first and third in the
hundred-metre sprint at school sports day.*

Damn it, I'm going to be late, Jess thought, as she grabbed
her keys and handbag and dashed out the door.

Parking outside the school gates, she saw the girls and
smiled. Her precious little poppet, so cute in her pigtails
and school dress that looked two sizes too big, with her
big sister holding on tightly to her hand.

The girls ran ahead, straight towards the playground,
their little bodies unable to contain the excitement of being
there first. By the time Jess caught up with them, they were
scrambling over monkey bars, riding up and down on the
seesaw, and jumping on and off swings at a speed that
would impress any mammalogist.

In no time at all, the playground was teaming with kids
enjoying after-school freedom with friends, while mums
were busy chatting and opening packets of biscuits and
buns to feed the hungry hordes.

Jess sat down on a bench, close enough to hear the other
mothers' conversations, but far enough away to not have to

engage in the comparative details of everyone's daily lives. Cloned in their latest Lorna Jane tights and quotable tank tops, the women looked like a murder of magpies, squawking their affirmations: *She believed she could so she did.*

Jess saw the familiar face of one of the mothers. Her long blonde hair was tied back in a ponytail, complementing her flawless features. Jess mused at the message on her top: *Today is a PERFECT DAY to start living your dreams. Make it happen.*

That feels like a blessing, Jess thought.

The sudden piercing squeals and screams drew Jess's attention back to the playground. She walked over to her girls. They were playing in the tower and had spotted her through the bright yellow telescope.

'Look out, someone's coming!' her little poppet squealed.

'Hey, there, what are you two playing?' asked Jess.

'We're playing princesses and trolls,' little poppet's big sister explained. 'The boys are the trolls, and we're the princesses.'

'And what beautiful princesses you are, too.' Jess took out her phone, zoomed in and clicked. Another perfect shot.

High-pitched squeals of fearful fun were set off again as the trolls started climbing the princesses' tower. Laughing, Jess sat back down, amused at the ferocity of the little princesses as they defended their castle.

She overheard a mother with *WILLPOWER* moralised across her top ask the flawless blonde, 'What stall are you working on at the fete, Bec?'

'Helping out with the cake stall again,' Bec replied. 'But I think they're a bit short of volunteers so I'll probably be there the whole time, which I don't mind. Better than following the kids around all day.'

'True, and at least they'll know where to find you.'

'Okay, you kids, you've got two minutes and then we're going. I want to make the four o'clock gym class,' Bec yelled at the playground.

'By the way, what are you doing tomorrow?' the other woman asked Bec. 'I thought a few of us could do lunch at Lutèce. I've heard the food is just fabulous and they've got a great wine selection, too.'

'Sounds great, the cleaner's coming tomorrow and she hates it when I'm hanging around the house. And if I have one too many wines she can probably pick up the kids, too,' Bec said with a laugh.

'That's a great idea, I might see if my babysitter can pick mine up, too.'

So much for *WILLPOWER*, thought Jess.

It was eight pm. The silence of the house wrapped around Jess like a tired old unwanted coat. She gently shut the bedroom door and went into her study. Picking up the silver-framed photo of the girls, Jess stared at them longingly, tenderly stroking their smooth glass cheeks. They smiled proudly back at her, holding up the medals they'd won at the school sports day. She remembered the excitement on their little faces as they ran across the finish line, oblivious to their first and third places. Memories of all those special moments she captured swiped through her mind, one photo at a time.

Jess took a glimpse at the clock: nine-thirty. Time had slipped silently past her again.

As usual, a lot had been happening on Facebook. Scrolling through the posts of online acquaintances and strangers, Jess wondered whether their lives were really that perfect.

So proud of my daughter Heidi! Just got a 1st for her ballet solo!

Coffee & cake, celebrating the boys making their first Communion.

Our first 11-week scan with Dr Lee.

Big Friday night for the Joneses! Downloading the Frozen soundtrack and having a dance and singalong with the kids. No one does a musical like Disney.

Nobody ever posts the negative truths of reality, she thought.

My daughter Heidi is in deep shit! Just caught her smoking pot in the backyard.

Coffee & cake, stuffing my face after finding out my husband's been screwing the next-door neighbour.

My first counselling session with Dr Lee.

Friday night on my own again. Downloading Notting Hill with a bottle of cab sav and a box of tissues. No one does a love story like Hugh Grant.

Jess uploaded her photos: *My beautiful princesses fighting off trolls!*

Waiting at the school gates near the Lorna Jane gang, Jess listened to the excited voices of the kids as they trailed out, minds and bodies miraculously full of boundless energy the teachers wished they'd had an hour ago. Jess kept her eyes focused on the P1–3 building, anticipating that first moment when the girls came around the corner and smiled.

Jess overheard one of the women ask Bec, 'So, who's looking forward to the fete tomorrow?'

'Not me,' groaned Bec. 'I'd been training for a triathlon, then realised it was the same weekend as the fete.'

How about *OBSESSED* for a new slogan, thought Jess, as she took out her phone, zoomed in and captured her two little princesses running towards her. Each moment was as precious as their every breath, and she didn't want to miss a single second.

It was a perfect day for the fete, the bright spring sunshine accentuating the vividness of a cloudless blue sky. Hundreds of children, parents, grandparents and others milled around the busy stalls and rides.

Jess saw some of the Lorna Jane gang sipping wine at the bar, seemingly oblivious to any thought or care of their kids' whereabouts. She headed down to the back of the oval, her arms loaded with a tempting array of treats: chocolate brownies, cupcakes, and two bright red slushies.

The girls should still be at the jumping castle, Jess thought, recalling last year when they went on it over and over and over again.

She searched for them in the long line-up of kids at the castle. They weren't there. She checked the merry-go-round, the cup and saucer, and the baby animal petting zoo. They were nowhere in sight. Jess felt her heart begin to race as she hurried along the stalls, past the lucky wheel and the laughing clowns, which appeared to mock her rising panic.

Then, breathing a silent prayer of relief, she found them at last. With their faces painted, they were barely recognisable. Her little princesses had been transformed into a rainbow butterfly and a brightly striped tiger.

'Wow, you girls look amazing,' Jess said breathlessly. 'Let me take a photo of the world's most beautiful butterfly and the jungle's scariest tiger. Perfect. I've brought some morning tea to share. Are you two hungry?'

'Yes,' they replied in unison.

'And I'm a bit thirsty, too,' replied her little poppet, eyeing off the slushie.

Jess smiled. 'Come on, then, let's go over there in the shade of the trees.'

'Bec, you have to see this,' called a woman, waving her phone in the air. 'I was just talking to Andrea and she said she saw photos of your girls on Facebook last night. Look, here are the girls from the playground this week, and here they are coming out of school. And look, here they are again at the sports day last month.'

It was a perfect day for the fete, the bright spring sunshine accentuating the vividness of a cloudless blue sky. Holding tightly to the hands of her two precious girls, Jess walked calmly out of the school grounds. She glanced down at her tank top and grinned.

DREAM. BELIEVE. ACHIEVE.

Mile High

Martii Maclean

'There's a life sign in the waste pod,' said Joe, as he switched on the pod camera.

'Well, yeah,' said Norris. 'Garbage men—sorry, waste monitors—have heartbeats, too.'

'Well, no. The pod doors are sealed and the cycle's started. No one should be in there.'

'Very bad for your health.' Norris pressed the alarm button.

Images from the waste pod wobbled and became solid on Joe's monitor. 'There's someone in there, all right. A female-shaped someone.'

Joe and Norris both turned towards the door as they heard the distinct clatter of Sally from sector security enter the control room. She wore archaic weaponry on a belt that rattled as she walked. A pistol and Taser jangled against antique handcuffs.

Joe raised an eyebrow. The show of arms was so last century, and no one in their right mind would use either weapon on Mile High. No one wanted any pesky holes shot through the walls and membranes they all relied on for staying alive. Air was thin and cold a mile up, and punctured dirigibles tended to make rude noises as they deflated and fell out of the sky. It was already risky enough that the city council let any tattered old airship that could make it to Mile High tether and join the city, and maybe burst, collapse and drag others down, without someone shooting holes all over the place.

It wasn't likely that Sally would shoot at anyone. There weren't any real crimes committed in Mile High, Joe thought, unless you counted Sally's crime against fashion. But he liked how she looked all the same. No, there was only one penalty for a crime in the floating city, and that was to strip the offender of their citizenship. Then they had to leave, walk the plank.

'So, what's happening?' Sally asked, as she leaned over Joe to get a look at the screen.

Joe could feel the cold metal of her pistol pressing into his back, and something warmer and softer press into his shoulder. Some days, being a garbage guy was great. 'Someone's in there.'

'So?' said Sally

'So, once the door is closed, the cycle starts automatically,' said Joe. 'She has about twenty-one minutes before she drops out when the floor opens to dump the rubbish.'

'Nasty, but not incorrect,' said Norris. 'Unless she can knit a parachute out of the trash in the pod in twenty minutes, she won't be alive to experience the wasteland wonders of the down under.'

'Twenty minutes and she'll fall ...' Sally leaned in again. 'You've got to be able to stop the cycle.'

'N-no,' stammered Joe. He struggled to concentrate on anything but the warm softness.

'So someone in Mile High is sending people to their deaths.' Sally stuck her thumbs into her weapon belt and turned to Norris. 'Who has clearance to start a cycle?'

'I'll get the names,' said Norris, leaving the control room. Sally leaned into Joe's shoulder again.

'Damn,' he mumbled.

'Damn what?'

'Um, damn I wish she'd turn around so I could see who she is.'

The figure on the screen was definitely female. She was standing, staring at the digits on the outer door's panel that were slowly counting down the remaining minutes — now eighteen — of the pod cycle and her life. She just stood there, frozen except for the occasional swaying nudge caused by the linked dirigibles that made up the floating city, bumping against each other as they travelled.

Joe had well-developed air legs, so normally he never noticed the nudging of the city's movements, but as he watched the girl sway now he could feel every minute jolt.

'Why isn't she panicking?' he said. 'I sure would be.'

'It doesn't make sense,' said Sally. 'I know all the troublemakers in this cluster and she's not one of them, so who would have a motive to kill her?'

'You sound like you fell out of an old movie.'

'Give a girl a break.' She punched him on the shoulder. 'Old detective movies are the closest thing I get to action in this drifting utopia.'

I'd help you find some action, thought Joe, but he just smiled to himself. 'Well, Sally, what do they say? Don't do the crime 'cause you'd never survive the climb ... down, that is.'

'I know. The idea of having to walk the plank is quite a deterrent.'

'If the only crime you see is in the old movies, why haven't you hung up your gunbelt?'

'Good thing I didn't, because someone did do the crime but now she'll be doing the climb.' Sally tapped the image of the girl on the monitor. 'You really can't open the door?'

'No.' Joe sighed and wiped beads of sweat from his top lip.

Sally walked over to look through the small window in the garbage-pod door. 'There's no sign of a scuffle. She's not tied up. She just seems to be waiting, accepting it.' Her shoulders sagged.

'Shouldn't there be some yelling or crying?' Joe stood and walked over to stand close to Sally. 'She's about to fall to her death and she's just staring at the countdown.'

'Sixteen minutes to go,' Sally whispered, and shuddered. 'We're looking at a murder being committed.'

'You okay?' Joe reached out and gripped Sally's shoulders, pulling her towards him.

'I don't know how much good this list will be,' said Norris, interrupting the moment, 'there's lots of names.'

Sally turned, pulling away from Joe's attempted comfort. 'Doesn't matter much unless someone on the list can halt the cycle.' She took the list and scanned it. 'You two are on here. Where were you guys about fifteen or so minutes ago?'

'We're garbage guys,' said Joe. 'The trash doesn't come to us, you know. We were doing the rounds.'

Norris nodded. 'Joe noticed the sensor as soon as we got back here.'

'And the others on the list?'

'Most of these are off shift.' Joe took hold of the list, and Sally's hand, then crossed off the names of those who were off shift hours ago.

'Fourteen minutes,' said Norris.

'I'm afraid her fate is as sealed as the pod door, but I still need to find out who coded the door closed in case they decide to do it to someone else.' Sally sighed deeply.

'The system will have a record of the code,' said Joe. 'But I don't have clearance to—'

'The codes! Thank you.' Sally kissed Joe hard on the mouth. 'I am embarrassingly out of practice at solving crimes. The system allocates everyone with an individual passcode.'

'Do you have access to them?' Joe gasped, his heart hammering.

Sally nodded and ran for the door, then stopped. 'Hey, Norris, double-check location logs to see where everyone on that list is, can you?'

'On it.'

'And Joe, can you ask coms why she might be wearing those earbuds? And that's no personal sound cube she's holding.'

Joe looked through the small window at the girl's profile. Now he could see that she was wearing tiny earbuds and holding a jerry-rigged bundle of wires. 'Good spotting.'

'That's what detectives do.' Sally gave a crooked, hopeful smile and disappeared.

Joe sent a request message to coms about the earbuds and then helped Norris firm up the location of everyone on the garbage list. 'Eleven minutes.'

'We're one short,' said Norris. 'Double-check me.'

'You're right, one short. Olga.' Joe flicked on the duty screen. 'She's off shift, but not logged into her quarters — or anyone else's.' He winked.

'I'll get someone in the lookout to watch for her.' Norris messaged across to the lookout in the central drift cluster, where off-duty workers usually gathered.

'Seven minutes,' said Joe.

Sally burst into the control room. 'I've got a password and a name. I know whose code it was.'

'Let's play snap,' said Joe. 'Your person is Olga.'

'Yep.'

'I have word from the lookout,' said Norris. 'It appears our Olga is standing, pressed up against the side widow and staring out, and has been for about twenty minutes.'

'How long does it take to walk from here to the lookout?' asked Sally.

Joe smirked. 'Less than ten minutes.'

'Nate in coms has replied about the earbuds,' said Norris. 'Weird, but I'll read what he says. "She's wearing buds because she's Milly, and that's what she always does." He's coming up.'

Nate appeared in the doorway and stared at the swaying figure in the trash pod. 'That's her, Milly. She's from coms, but in another drift cluster. She transferred a couple of weeks ago and has worn the earbuds almost all the time since she arrived. She likes to tinker with the dodgy old com-links.'

'She's still got the bundle of wires.'

'Do you know what she's listening to?' Sally asked Nate.

'I thought she was chatting with that strange pale girl she spends time with, the one who never talks to anyone else. It didn't seem to stop her working, so I ignored it.'

'That must be Olga,' said Sally.

'That's the name,' said Nate.

'What, Olga locked Milly in and is taunting her via some cobbled com-link while she waits for her to die?' said Joe.

'Why would she do that if they're friends?' asked Norris.

'Jealousy? Maybe Milly was using the radio to whisper sweet nothings to Olga's fella.' Joe laughed. 'Just like in the old movies.'

'Five minutes.' Norris shook his head.

Nate stared at his shoes and held a headphone tightly to one ear as the scanner searched each frequency. He looked at Sally. 'She's listening to an external signal.'

'What?'

'Someone down under is talking to her.'

'More questions than answers.' Sally rubbed her temples. 'Why did Olga want Milly in a garbage pod? And how did she force her to get inside?'

'I *didn't*. Hey, go easy, you gorilla.'

They turned and saw a broad-shouldered lookout bouncer shoving a small, sullen-faced young woman through the door.

'You must be Olga,' said Sally.

Olga nodded stiffly and yanked her arm free of the bouncer.

'Three minutes,' Norris mumbled through his teeth.

'The passcode log shows that you started the pod cycle,' Sally said. Another stiff nod. 'Why?'

'Milly begged me to.'

'Crap,' said Sally. 'You're saying she asked you to help her kill herself, and you said yes?'

'Nope, weirder ... she wants to leave.'

'You're joking,' said Joe.

'Does this look like a comedy face to you?' Olga said. 'Look, I really want to go back to the window so I can see if she makes it. Then you can charge me and make me walk the plank. I just want to see if it was all bullshit.'

'If what was bullshit?' said Sally.

'I've known Milly since school, back when we were on the starboard drift cluster. She always liked the coms stuff. She had this hobby, building devices, and then she got curious to know if there were any signals coming from down under. Then she heard—met—Thomas and ... I don't get it, but they seem to have fallen in love.' She shrugged. 'I reminded her what things were supposed to be like down under, but she believed what he told her and decided to switch teams to be with him.'

'Well, there isn't going to be much of a romantic moment once the pod opens,' said Sally.

'Thomas said he'd be waiting for her with some gear to soften her landing,' Olga said.

'Right,' scoffed Norris. 'Mile High has a random trajectory. It stops all the down-low trash knowing where we'll be and trying to attack us.'

'It's all random except for one place,' said Olga.

'Crossing the mountains,' mumbled Nate, as he put the headphones down. 'Because of some of the old, smaller airships that have joined the city, we can only go so high. There's only one place we can traverse this mountain range, one non-random location. Sometimes we barely clear it by five decimetres.'

'And the trash down there knows about it?' Norris shook his head.

'They're not stupid,' said Olga.

'So this Thomas knew when we'd be passing,' said Norris.

'No, but he knew we would. He just watched out for us and told Milly when we were close.' Olga walked over and lightly touched her friend's image on the screen. 'That's when she asked for my help.'

There was a creaking screech as the floor began to slide open. Joe and Sally pushed their faces close to the tiny window. They could see patches of blue in places where the rubbish had already fallen away. Then they saw Milly, smiling, as she dropped from sight.

Murder on the Mountain

A Jack Harrigan Thriller

Paul Smith

The afternoon mist engulfed the mountain resort as the mercury dropped below five degrees. Jenny and I had nestled ourselves at a small table by the fireplace and I was enjoying the warmth of the Bundy rum sliding down my throat. We had driven two busloads of budding authors to the annual rainforest writers' retreat, which my daughter had been running for four years.

Several members of the group were enjoying a drink. I could see Bev Walterson and her daughter over by the window with Debby Dallas. Peter Elsom, a rough-looking bloke, looked out of place among the budding authors attending the workshop. Peter had given one of the young barmen a hard time the day before, proving himself to be a bully. Kate Donavan, my good drinking partner, waved from the bar, a spot she was well acquainted with.

My appreciation of the view through the French doors was rudely interrupted as my daughter Clementine pushed her way towards us. She was supporting an injured man. It was Tom Beatie, who was looking the worse for wear. Blood was trickling down his face and he was limping. Tom, a well-known crime-fiction writer, was one of the guest speakers, and wasn't due to leave until tomorrow afternoon.

'Dad, you have to come, there's been an accident. Marlene Drake has run off the road.'

'What the hell were they doing? That road would be as slippery as buggery after all this rain.'

'She was taking me down to Canungra when we went off the road,' said Tom.

'Is she all right?'

'No, she's in a bad way,' Tom said. 'I couldn't get her out of the car. I think she might be dead.'

'How on earth did you make it back up here? You look a mess.'

'I walked,' he said, as he collapsed into a chair.

'Okay, Clementine, you get Tom fixed up and call an ambulance. Jenny and I will go down and see what we can do.'

I had been a private detective for more than forty years, and three years ago I had put Jenny on as my assistant. She handed me the car keys and we headed for the door. I looked back at Tom. I could tell that his suave good looks would be seriously at risk after this.

The SUV was parked out front, so Jenny and I climbed aboard and made our way down to the crash site, following the steep road that wound around the mountain. Jenny was first to spot the broken trees and tyre tracks veering off the tight bend on a hairpin curve. The steep road had been partially washed away, dropping down to rocks and forest below.

It had been a pretty scary road before the damage— coming up, I had held my breath every time an oncoming car had to pass—but now it was downright insanity to drive up here before the road crew could make repairs. Three kilometres out, the incline became increasingly steep, and, as if things weren't tricky enough, water was now cascading across what was left of the asphalt surface.

The SUV slipped sideways, and I increased the throttle just enough to gain traction. The afternoon sun broke through the mist, causing a rainbow to appear, but there was no pot of gold at the end of this one, only a fifty-metre drop.

Thankfully, the road here was in good shape, and it even had a section to allow another vehicle to pass. I pulled up as close as I could to the edge and got out to assess the situation. The wreck was twenty metres down, wrong side up and pinned against a ghost gum. Getting to it was going to be difficult due to the steepness of the slope and damp footing, so I told Jenny to stay with the car.

After a few near tumbles, I finally reached the wreck and immediately realised there was nothing I could do for Marlene. Her head was crushed between the door and the roof of the four-wheel drive, and what seemed to be several litres of blood had pooled on the ground.

I saw a black leather satchel, which must have fallen out of the car, lying wedged between some grass tufts. I picked it up and opened it; inside was a manuscript and a memory stick. I tucked the satchel under my arm and was just about to head back up the slope when I smelled something vaguely familiar. Brake fluid.

On closer inspection, I found that the front, flexible brake line was leaking through a slit. This wasn't a case of a faulty component; it was a neat cut. This was not an accident. It was murder most foul.

When I made it back up to the road, Jenny was taking shots of tyre tracks with her phone. I shook my head in answer to the obvious question and we got back in the car. After turning the SUV around to face back up the mountain, I got out and checked the surface of the road for skid marks, of which there were none.

It took another thirty minutes for the ambulance to arrive, and it was the only other vehicle desperate enough to try the road in these conditions. I pointed to where the wreck was and they made their way down to the site. We left them to it.

Once back at the resort, I considered the facts. Investigating crimes was not new to me.

Marlene Drake, a regular attendee of the retreat, had not been very popular with the women in our group. One probable reason was that whenever someone nervously shared their writing in a workshop, Marlene would make snide remarks. She was a loud person anyway, and this was a way of gaining attention. She also seemed to consider every male as a possible sexual quest, regardless of his marital status. In fact, if a man came with a spouse, she'd circle like a hungry shark.

She wasn't hard on the eyes, and that glint of mischief could be an enticing elixir, but I surmised within minutes of first meeting Marlene that any close encounter would end in drama. And that was her genre: drama with a subplot of drama.

But killing her? That was stretching things a bit.

Maybe Marlene wasn't the intended victim.

I hadn't known Tom Beatie for long, but I had liked him right away. He was a good bloke, and one of Australia's best crime writers. I wouldn't have figured him for the type to make a Marlene mistake. I hadn't spotted any sparks between the two of them; I've got a nose for players, and as far as I could tell he wasn't one.

Before I went to see how Tom was, there was something I had to do.

Detective Inspector Des Corrington was head of the Gold Coast Crime Investigation Branch. We had clashed a few times over the years. He could be abrasive and pig-headed, but Des had a gone out on a limb for me more than once, and I thought I owed him a call to give him a heads-up.

I found Tom Beatie in the bar nursing a large whisky. He had a bandage wrapped around his head, but the injury wasn't as bad as it had first looked.

Lloyd, the barman (ever since seeing *The Shining*, for me all dedicated barmen are called Lloyd), had a Bundy and coke lined up for me. 'This one's on the house.'

Drink in hand, I approached Tom. 'Mind if I join you?'

'Yeah, sure, Jack, not that I'll be much company. Clementine told me you went down to the crash. I feel so bad having to leave Marlene like that, but there wasn't anything I could do.'

I slid the satchel over to him. 'I believe this is yours.'

He just nodded and took another sip.

'Your latest book?'

'My publisher has been screaming for it.' He went quiet and rubbed his damaged forehead. 'It's my fault that poor woman is dead, and just because there was a fucking deadline to meet.'

I took a healthy slug of the Bundy. 'So that's why you were headed down the mountain. Couldn't you have emailed it?'

'The bloody internet has been down ever since we got here. Canungra is the nearest place I could shoot it off from, and I was going to drive myself but the rental wouldn't have made it. Marlene offered to take me since she had a four-wheel drive. I can't understand it. The Lexus seemed to be handling the conditions, but then Marlene lost control for no apparent reason, and on a better part of the road.'

I leaned forward so not to be overheard. 'Tom, is there any reason someone would want you dead?'

'No, of course not.' He looked hard at me. 'You don't think this was an accident, do you?'

'I *know* it wasn't, but keep that to yourself for the moment. I'm going to find out who's responsible.'

'Your daughter told me that you're a PI. I'd be obliged if you would take on the case.'

He agreed to my rates, and I told him that Jenny would bring a contract for him to sign. Things had been slow lately, so being paid to do what I was going to do anyway made good sense. After two days' break, I was back on the job.

'How well did you know Marlene?' I asked Tom.

'She and her husband run a small publishing business in Crows Nest. She was trying to get me to publish through their house.'

'Were you going to?'

'With all due respect for the dead, I wouldn't touch it with a ten-foot barge pole. Their business, Force Press, has a terrible reputation.'

'So you reckon they're a bit dodgy, then.'

'Yes, they target budding authors who have been rejected by the mainstream publishers, promise them the world, and then bleed them dry.'

'So it stands to reason she would have a few enemies.'

'A bloody long list, if you ask me, and rumour has it that she was blackmailing some high-profile media magnate.'

'Thanks, Tom, that's given me something to work on. Your glass is empty, what's your poison?'

'Jameson's on the rocks,' he said. 'Thanks, Jack.'

I excused myself to call Vinnie, who ran our Sydney branch of Harrigan Investigations.

He picked up after four rings. 'What's up, Jack?'

'Are you still in the office?'

'Yeah, sure, what can I do for you?'

'Can you check out Force Press, it's a publishing business over at Crows Nest.'

'I thought you were taking a break in some mountain retreat.'

'I was, but there's been a death and somehow the word "accident" is not sitting right with me. The name's Marlene Drake. Find out what you can about her and her husband.'

'I've heard of her. There was a scandal a few months ago involving Peter Goldberg, you know, the guy who's big in television and radio production. It was in all the gossip columns down here. His wife and Marlene had an altercation after the Logie awards.'

'Let me know what you can dig up. The internet's down at the moment due to a storm, but they expect to have it back up by tomorrow morning. In the meantime I'm reachable by mobile.'

As soon as I hung up, my mobile rang again. Des Corrington from CIB was on the line. He told me he and his forensics team would be catching a chopper in the morning and asked if I would be available to brief him, knowing that I would be sniffing around. I agreed to meet him at eight am, and told him I'd organise the resort's all-wheel-drive bus to take his team to the crash site.

Jenny and Clementine met me in the dining room for dinner, along with the rest of our group. Not surprisingly, Marlene's misfortune was the topic of conversation. I didn't air my suspicions, or try to question anyone, as I thought it best to leave that to Des.

I could then go about my own investigation without alarming anyone. One thing I did pick up through the table conversation was that there wouldn't be too many tears shed for the dear departed.

Only a handful of us seasoned drinkers adjourned to the bar, and I was pleased to see that Tom had retired early. I wasn't sure how he would have handled question time from the writers group after the shock of the accident, plus the effects of the whiskey.

I'd met Kate Donovan four years ago at the resort. She was a successful author who had helped Clementine set up the first workshop. Kate was about sixty, and could still turn heads with that buxom figure of hers. She knew everyone in the writing scene, and had a good nose for bullshit. I ordered a bottle of good sauvignon blanc and joined her at her table after the others had left.

She welcomed me and said, 'Top shelf, eh. I guess you're here for the lowdown on Marlene.'

'It might help.'

'Well, she teamed up with Simon, her husband, about twelve years back. He'd made a small fortune publishing celebrity cookbooks, even had his own TV show. She promoted budding authors who had more money than talent, and most did quite well. As for Simon and Marlene, theirs was a marriage of convenience. Simon's not really into women, if you get my drift.'

'I remember him from the workshop, a tubby little bloke with immaculate hair who always wore a bowtie.'

'That's him. He could be a nasty little prick at times. I had to stop my hubby from decking him at some fundraising event once. His shining light has faded lately. He had a couple of gigs with one of those reality-TV cooking shows, but he was demonstrating non-stick frypans, last I heard. Marlene is a goer, but the even the dumb rich wise up eventually. Simon and Marlene have an understanding, though. He has his expensive boys, and she bonks anyone who can put business her way.'

'So you don't think he could be the jealous type,' I said.

'Not a chance,' Kate said. 'If anything, he'd encourage her. I know that look, Jack. You think there's something fishy about the crash, don't you?'

'Just a hunch, but let's just keep it between us, okay?'

'Yeah, sure, but you might want to speak with Debby Dallas. I believe she and Marlene went to boarding school together.'

Back in our room, I made some notes before drifting into a restless sleep.

After an early breakfast, I spoke to the duty manager about using the bus for the forensic team. The police chopper put down next to the replica Stinson plane near the guesthouse and Des stepped out, rubbing his huge paws. It was a freezing morning, and I could see that he was even grumpier than usual.

'Where's this fucking bus, Harrigan?'

Two tall men in their thirties stepped out of the chopper. One was blond and Nordic looking, and the other could have been an Islander. The men were joined by an attractive blonde woman in her early forties.

'Awaiting your command, my lordship,' I said to Des.

He directed his team to go down to the site, and told them he would join them later.

'You look like you could use a coffee, Des,' I said. 'Come on, I'll let you know what I have.'

'I could use a fucking drink, but coffee will have to do. You're like that bloody Jessica Fletcher—a murder magnet. I reckon I'll find out it was you all along.'

'You've got me cold there, Des, but now you'll have to let those you've convicted out of prison. And they'll sue you for sure.'

'One day that smartarse mouth of yours is going to get you in deep shit, Harrigan.'

I lifted my hand to the scar on my forehead and said, 'Too late.'

In the cafe, Des took notes without comment as I filled him in on the information I had gathered. I'd just finished when his mobile rang.

He answered in monotone syllables, hung up and said, 'Simon Drake's, the deceased's husband, is flying up to Southport this morning, and I've arranged an interview for four pm.'

'I wouldn't mind sitting in on that,' I said. 'My bloke Vinnie in Sydney is doing a bit of snooping around on the guy.'

'Yeah, I suppose you can come in as a consultant. Make sure your bloke doesn't get caught doing anything illegal, he's a dodgy bastard if there ever was one.'

'But a most effective dodgy bastard, you must agree.'

'Okay, can you get me down to the crash site?'

'No worries,' I said. 'Wait here while I borrow an SUV.'

I phoned Vinnie from the car park; there was no way I wanted Des to hear this conversation. 'Vinnie, Simon Drake is coming up here, so his house should be empty. Maybe a courier-delivery cover would do the job.'

'What are you looking for?'

'Creditors' correspondence, bank statements ... oh, and see if you can dig up any insurance policies.'

'Yeah, no problem, I'll send anything I find to your mobile.'

Jenny was at the cafe when I picked up Des, so I asked her to pull Debby Dallas aside and sound her out about her friend Marlene.

We made the site without incident, although Des seemed a little nervous. His forensic team was hard at it. The blond copper, whose name was Ericsson, was checking the point where the vehicle had left the road.

Des and I made our way down the hill to the wreck. Lamb, the other policeman, was perched on top of the upside-down chassis inspecting the brake lines.

'These brake lines have definitely been tampered with,' he said, as we approached. 'There are incisions on both of the driver's-side flexible lines.'

'It's doubtful, but see if you can get any prints,' said Des, as he passed up a metal case.

'Hang on, I've found something here.' Lamb leaned down to make a closer inspection of the inner front mudguard. He removed a dark length of thread that looked like wool. He handed it to Des, who bagged it.

The blonde woman was inside the vehicle, scraping blood samples. I found out later that her name was Chris Parker, and she was a blood-splatter specialist consultant with Crime Investigation Branch.

The team spent another hour poking around, and then we all packed into the SUV and headed back up the mountain. Des directed the team to take the chopper back to the station, and told them he would call when he wanted to be picked up.

I drove him down to the conference centre just as the writers' group was breaking for morning tea. Des had met my daughter Clementine when she had helped me with several cases in the past, and he pulled her aside for a chat, but not before grabbing a coffee and three chocolate brownies.

Clementine announced to the group that Detective Inspector Corrington would be speaking to each member of the group individually as soon as tea break finished.

'Mr Beatie, I'd like to talk to you first,' Des said, 'so bring your coffee and we'll go out to the foyer. By the way, I just finished *I Can See You*.'

'What did you think?' Tom said to Des, looking pleased that the detective inspector had read his book.

'Loved the twist at the end,' Des said, 'I was sure it was the bikie.'

'Funny you should say that,' Tom said, 'so did I.'

Des raised an eyebrow and they left the hall.

I signalled to Jenny, and asked her, 'How did you go with Debby?'

'She's a timid little thing. I think Marlene used her as a gofa. They met at St Bridget's boarding school and had been friends ever since. Debby was going to be Marlene's bridesmaid twenty years ago, but Marlene's boyfriend died in a car accident. Marlene was badly injured and spent months recuperating. Debby said it changed her personality completely; that's when she became a go-getter and a bitch.'

'So the boyfriend died in the accident. It could be a motive if she was to blame, but why wait twenty years? I don't suppose you managed to get his name.'

'Give me some credit, Jack. Bill Walterson, and he was a motor mechanic from Dunedin in New Zealand. They met on a cruise. They had a flat in Harboard, in Sydney's north side.'

'Walterson ... hang on, that's Bev's surname, you know, the woman who comes here every year with her daughter, Roslyn.'

'Yeah, she's from Dunedin, too,' said Jenny, as she poured two glasses of cab sav.

'I must have a word with Bev; this is becoming interesting.'

'Oh, there's one other thing. When Marlene told Debby that she was taking Tom Beatie to Canungra, that big Lebanese-looking bloke was hanging about earwigging.'

I opened my briefcase and took out the list of people in the writers' group. 'Here he is, Peter Elsom, I saw him in the bar earlier. He looks like a real loner, that one.'

It was just before lunch break when I caught up with Des, who was finishing up an interview. 'Have you spoken to Bev Walterson yet?'

He looked at his list. 'No, she's next.'

'Do you mind if I sit on in this one? Her husband, Bill Walterson, was Marlene's fiance. They were in a car crash twenty years ago, and he died. Given that he and Bev are both from Dunedin, he could've been her son or younger brother.'

'Yeah, sure, that could be relevant.'

When asked about Bill's death, Bev said that Marlene had not been responsible for the accident. He had been driving, and a truck crossed double lines.

Most of the members of the group were out in the courtyard when we finished Bev's interview, milling around the sandwich-laden trestle tables. The topic of conversation centred on Marlene's death, and I heard some interesting but preposterous theories. Des had interviewed about half of the group and was now stuffing food down his gob at an alarming rate. He wasn't a small lad, and it was easy to see how he'd got that way.

I sought out Clementine and asked her about Peter Elsom, the loner from the bar.

'He was the last person to book in and specified a villa, even though he's by himself.'

'Does anyone in the group seem to know him?' I asked.

'No, he keeps to himself. In fact, I'm not sure why he's here since he hasn't taken much interest in the workshops.'

'How did he pay?'

She went to her satchel and riffled through some papers. 'Direct deposit from Concord Security.'

'Interesting. I've heard of them, there was something in the paper about links to a bikie gang.'

Jenny gave me the number of his villa, and I told her to let Des know that I was going to check out Peter Elsom.

He was in the process of loading his luggage into the back of a Ford Territory. He was about six feet tall, big but going to fat, with longish, greasy receding hair and a handlebar moustache.

'Leaving us so quickly, Mr Elsom?'

'What's it to you?'

'I think the detective inspector might want a word with you. It seems you're the number one candidate for Marlene Drake's murder.'

'Yeah? Well, he can go fuck himself, and so can you.'

He was a lot quicker than he looked. He spun around and let go a haymaker, which I only just managed to duck. He continued to charge at me, throwing punches as he came.

Back in the seventies, I was with an elite military unit and was highly trained in most forms of martial art, all of which I now totally ignored. Ducking under one of his blows, I moved in and drove my forehead into his nose, following up with a knee to the family jewels that lifted him off the ground. Stepping off to the right, I put all of my eighty-five kilos behind a right cross to his jaw and he slumped to the ground, lights out.

A gravelly voice called out behind me, 'I suppose you learned that in the special forces.'

'No, Detective Inspector, Redfern Primary School.'

'That'd be right. You could've left him conscious. How am I supposed to question him now?'

'He'll wake up, eventually.'

Jenny walked over to me. 'You're too old for this shit, Jack. Give me a look at that hand, and your head is bleeding like a stuck pig.'

She was right. The middle knuckle was split open, and the one behind the little finger had been driven back an inch. My head was okay, but I do bleed a lot, being on blood thinners and aspirin.

We left Des to take charge of the suspect and went back to our room to get me cleaned up. I knew I was in for a lecture. Jenny was right, I was getting too old for this shit. My busted paw hurt like buggery. She took away some of the pain with some ice, a kiss and a healthy dash of Bundy and coke, but a phone call spoiled the moment.

It was Vinnie. He had found correspondence from creditors indicating that the Drakes were up to their eyeballs in debt, and a new insurance policy on Marlene for one million dollars. When I phoned Des on his mobile and passed on the information, he had the good grace not to ask me how I came across it.

Two hours later, Des phoned and asked me to come back to the conference centre so he could take a statement.

'Good work, Jack,' he said. 'I found a blue jumper in Elsom's gear that matches the thread from the wreck. He's singing like a canary, reckons Drake paid him fifteen thousand dollars to knock off his old lady. It's a wonder he can still talk. He spat out three teeth, and I think you broke his jaw.'

'What about Simon Drake?' I asked.

'We'll pinch him when he comes in this afternoon.'

'Good, she may have been a bitch, but she didn't deserve to die.'

'Yeah, you're right. The road's open now so we have a car on its way. We'll have this thing wrapped up by the end of the day.'

My PI licence was under suspension for the use of excessive force against a paedophile a few months back, so I seized the opportunity to score some brownie points. 'About my licence hearing, Des, old mate.'

'You don't miss a trick, do you, Jack? Come in and pick it up next week. You can shout me lunch. Got to go, there's my lift now.'

Tom Beatie was shaking his head and smiling. 'Don't forget to send me a bill,' he said to Des. 'It'll be worth it. I reckon there's a book in this.'

'A book about me? Don't be ridiculous.'

Problem Solver

Kathy Childs

My shadow casts a silhouette, imitating a body prone across the steps that lead up to the office. I focus on the shadow, watching it expand, misshape, and re-form as I pull open the door and enter the warmth. The office upstairs is full of early-morning noises, the clatter of coffee cups competing with the voices of my colleagues as they attempt to gain kudos by reimagining their lives, truth spiced with inventiveness and wishful thinking.

I place a booted foot on the bottom stair and begin my ascent, my bag jolting on my hip in time with the movement. My palm glides up the wooden handrail as I climb. I run my fingers back and forth across a hollow, a minor dent. I caress the wood.

'Oh my god, Sue! We didn't expect you in today.'

'What are you doing here?'

'Oh, Susan dear, how are you coping?'

The gossip vultures perch, waiting. Whatever I say, how I say it, what my face betrays; all will be swiftly devoured. I am newsworthy and they are after the scoop.

'I don't want to talk about it.' I inch away.

'But Terry's dead.'

'I know.' I drag my hands through my hair, pushing it off my face.

'Oh, honey. It's a shock to all of us, but you saw him fall. Were there when he died. It has to be hard being back here at all.'

'They said he tripped on his shoelace and fell head first.'

A steaming hot cup is pushed into my hand. I bring it to my nose and inhale the fragrance of freshly brewed coffee. No one has ever made me coffee before. I nod a thank-you.

'Is that what happened?' Coffee Girl wants something for her efforts.

'I saw him falling.' I close my eyes. Bow my head.

'And you ran down the stairs and got to him. What then?' Coffee Girl pauses. 'Did he say anything?'

Breaths are collectively held.

'He said'— I look up—'I can't move my legs.'

'That's because his neck was broken, wasn't it?' says Junior Gossip, whose housemate is a nurse. 'Was his neck swollen at all? It's often a sign of a break, you know.'

'It's possible,' I say.

'You probably shouldn't have moved him.'

'I was just trying to see if he was hurt.'

'And he was, wasn't he?' No sorrow, just malicious interest.

'Yes, he was.'

'And then?'

The vultures lean forward, angling, necks craned so as not to miss a word.

'The guy from next door arrived and called an ambulance. While he was gone, Terry died.' I sit at my desk, turn on my computer and sip my coffee as the system boots up.

From behind me, the collective sighs.

'How awful,' Coffee Girl says.

I loved my job once. Under my old boss, Marcia, I had been challenged, encouraged, appreciated. But motherhood beckoned and Marcia deserted me. Terry, our new manager, was of a different ilk: part weasel, part snake. I'm sure he pictured himself as the stocky AFL ruck man he had been fifteen years ago and not the reality of a balding thirty-five year old running to flab. He had no concept of personal space; he stood way too close, his sweaty hands forever touching, caressing, stroking.

I'd been quite far down the line for his advances, given my small size and non-existent bust. Terry might have passed me by except for my long blonde hair, which seemed to intrigue him. He made a habit of running his damp fingers through my hair as he walked past my desk.

He cornered me one afternoon in the tearoom; standing behind me, he'd grabbed my breast, squeezing it like you would an avocado to see if it was ripe.

'Suppose more than a handful's a waste.'

'Piss off, Terry.' I pulled my elbow back hard, slamming into his stomach.

'Bitch.' He leaned in close and I could feel his hot, salami tainted breath on my neck. 'Redundancies next week, would be tough for you to lose your job. I know you need it.' And then he pushed his groin into my back, forcing me against the kitchen bench. 'Just a little fun and you might even get a raise. Any more of your smart-aleck talk and you're out.' He ground his hips hard against me.

Pushing back wasn't an option; I knew that would just encourage him.

'Think about it, but not for too long.' He patted my behind, chuckled and left.

I placed both hands on the bench to steady myself, took a deep breath and shuddered.

I'm a solo mum with a mortgage, and part-time positions are impossible to find. I need this job. I don't have the luxury of walking away like Hilary. Terry was one of the boys; reporting him would have found me in the queue at Centrelink like Chloe: redundant with no reference.

I am not like Hilary or Chloe. I do not run and I do not confront.

Yesterday I'd been tied up in a teleconference in the meeting room. When I surfaced, it was late and the office was deserted. I made it to the landing at the top of the stairs before Terry caught up with me. He grabbed a handful of my hair, yanked hard. His stale breath hissed as he leaned in, suggesting a detour to the storeroom on our way out; a little privacy.

He ran his sweaty fingers through my hair, tugged at the strands, forcing my head towards him, then smirked as he reminded me about the redundancies next week. He released my hair, but then grabbed my backside, his large hands squeezing and kneading, his lips making disgusting smacking noises.

There was no real thought behind it. I simply stuck out my booted foot and tripped Terry as he went to take his first step down towards the seclusion of the storeroom.

I observed dispassionately as he tumbled down the stairs, his head striking the anti-slip edging. I was surprised by how little sound it made. I watched as he grabbed for the handrail, his pinky ring denting the soft wood as his grip missed.

I waited for a while after the final thud and then strolled down, step by slow, deliberate step, boots clunking on the wood, down to where he had stopped, sprawled hard against the glass door.

'That was deliberate. You bitch.' He moaned and his body slumped. 'I'll have you for this.' I could hear the agony in his voice.

I watched the blood ooze from his battered nose, a river of red dripping from his flabby jowls, spreading across his white shirtfront.

'What's wrong with you? Call an ambulance.'

A rap on the glass door intruded into my stupor.

'Is he okay?' The tech head from next door peered in.

'Can you call an ambulance? You'll need to wait at the gate and direct them in. I'll stay with him.'

'Okay.' And off he ran, hitting triple zero on his phone as he faded into the darkness.

I knelt beside Terry's prone body, cradling his oversized head in my lap. His breathing was laboured. 'Am I going to be made redundant next week?'

'Redundant? Not likely. I'm going to sue you for assault. Redundancy will seem like a dream.' Spittle flew from his lips.

I stroked his double chins, my fingers absently caressing the stubble.

'Now the bitch gets friendly. You'll have to do better than that to get out of this one.'

I positioned my hand under his clammy neck, seeking a place among the folds of flesh. He grimaced as I adjusted my position. My right hand firmly grasped his chin, my left moved higher up now on the back of the head. A gentle movement to the left and then a sharp one to the right. There was an almost indiscernible crack.

I laid his head gently on the floor and moved towards his feet. After a sideways glance to confirm that the tech guy was still out of sight I yanked hard on one shoelace. I perched on the bottom step, composed my face in sorrow.

The paramedics found me there, sitting on the stairs, my head bowed and resting on my hands, a study in grief.

I sit at my desk this morning waiting for the obligatory emotions to hit. Instead of remorse, guilt and shame, I feel elation. I take a deep breath and the air that fills my lungs tastes of champagne and bubbles.

I silently toast my mother. It was she who told me that the difference between who you are and who you want to be lies in what you do.

Hilary ran away.

Chloe believed in fighting for what was right regardless of the cost.

Me? I'm a problem solver.

Smithy

Chris Radge

'That's a new one.' Detective Constable Jeffery Ryan turned to his superior.

'Agreed. I thought I'd seen it all in this job.' Detective Sergeant Matt McKay pulled out his phone to take a photo.

'How the hell are they going to get that croc off the vic?' Ryan's hand shaded his eyes from the relentless North Queensland sun. 'It's straddling the body like a bucking bull at a rodeo.'

'No friggin' idea.' McKay shook his head. He was glad he'd grabbed his mirrored sunnies from the squad car. 'The croc experts better get here soon, it doesn't look like it's leaving in a hurry.'

'I don't understand why it's just lying there.' Ryan took a step closer to the edge of the dune. 'Usually the vic'd be chomped by now, or at the very least dragged into the water, tumbled and left to rot under a submerged tree.' He tumbled his hands like a dance move from *Saturday Night Fever*.

'Got me beat. One for the forensics team, I reckon. First we need to find out who it is.'

'The croc's lying on his face, making it hard to see.' Ryan squinted at the scene.

McKay just nodded.

'I'm not going down there to find out who it is just yet.' Ryan pointed to where the crocodile was on the beach. 'These are brand spanking new Oxfords my wife bought me. I'll be deader than the vic if I so much as scuff 'em.'

McKay laughed, looking at Ryan's shiny black shoes. 'Are you going to click your heels three times, Dorothy?'

'Dumb arse, hers were red,' Ryan said, and gave his partner a gentleman's shove. It was just hard enough and close enough to the edge of the dune for him to lose his own balance as the sand dune collapsed under him. 'Farrrrrrrrrk.'

McKay whipped out a hand, latched onto his partner's forearm and heaved him backwards. 'Those shoes are going to need a spit and polish,' he said, as he watched Ryan tip the sand out of them. 'Me, I like my high tops, doesn't matter where I go.'

They heard the rumble of an engine, and a truck with pictures of crocodiles on the side rolled to a stop a few metres away from the detectives.

'Now the action's about to start,' McKay said. 'I just hope the crime scene isn't too badly disturbed before we get a chance to get down there.' He turned to one of the men grabbing equipment from the back of the truck. 'Hey, do your best not to disturb too much on or around the body.'

'Yeah, mate, we *always* do our best with crocs or someone might not go home.'

'True enough,' McKay said.

The crocodile experts stood on the edge of the dune and assessed the unusual crime scene.

Ryan let out a long whistle. 'Geeez, they're kitted out.'

Each specialised belt was stocked with high-quality silver gaffer tape, a canvas bag that looked like it would easily fit over a crocodile's head, a coiled rope with a lasso at one end, a fully loaded tranquiliser gun capable of subduing a crocodile, and a large knife protected by a thick leather cover.

It was time to get the big reptile, which was lying on the corpse, under control, but first they had to lightly tranquilise the animal or it could get ugly. The shot was true: a perfect hit near the crocodile's main artery. Anywhere else and it wouldn't have penetrated the leathery skin. The serum entered the animal's system quickly and its movements slowed. They waited until the head spotter gave the all clear to proceed, extending one arm straight up and signalling like an aircraft marshaller.

'Here we go,' said McKay in a hushed tone.

It was almost silent now except for the waves lapping on the beach.

The heaviest crocodile catcher lined himself up behind the partially sedated reptile. He had to launch himself up and over the victim, and the crocodile, to make it far enough to get to the snout safely. Even though the crocodile had been tranquilised it had taken fifteen minutes to set up everything, and he knew that the potency of the tranquiliser had lessened.

The catcher had done this plenty of times. No time like the present, he thought. He sailed through the air and landed squarely on the crocodile's back.

Ccccccrack.

A gurgling roar that sounded like it could have come from a T rex broke the silence.

Everyone froze except for the catcher on top of the crocodile, who had no time to check what the noise was; he had a snapping front end and lashing tail to contend with. It was manic. The reptile's head snapped from side to side, desperate to rid itself of the human on its back, and also raise itself off the other one underneath.

'We've got blood!' yelled Spence, the spotter. 'Looks like it's comin' from the dead guy's head.' The crocodile stood up and Spence yelled, 'No, it's comin' from the reptile.'

Streams of blood could be clearly seen underneath the base of the crocodile's tail.

'Shit, what's that from?' Spence said. 'No wonder the croc's agitated. Get that head under control and then we'll deal with it.'

Three catchers expertly lassoed the tail and head, rodeo style.

'Pull the rope tight, quick,' Spence said.

It did the trick, but they wound the rope around the snout a few more times to be sure.

'Right, get the gaffer on quick, fellas,' Spence said.

The crocodile was still doing its best to get off the victim; its tail was thrashing so much the catchers had to lasso it with a second rope to keep it still enough to finish. But the situation was still too dangerous.

'Best tranq him again, I reckon,' Spence said. 'Put him out properly.' He pulled the tranquiliser gun from his belt. It would be a difficult shot. Miss and he risked hitting the catcher on the crocodile's back, which would probably mean his death because the potency of the tranquiliser was double this time. But if he didn't fire, it would be the man's death anyway.

Spence got as close as safely possible, steadied his stance and *phwt*, the dart sailed past the crocodile's head by mere millimetres and landed squarely in the leather of the knife sheath belonging to Joe, one of the catchers.

'Jesus, sorry, mate,' Spence said, 'the sand gave way.'

Joe scowled as he plucked out the tranquiliser dart and placed it safely in the sheath with his knife.

Reloading, Spence knew this was his last round. He took aim, dug his feet deeply into the sand and watched the crocodile until tunnel vision took over. The shot sank into the reptile's flesh. There was a gurgle that sounded like the low roar of a lion and then the crocodile slumped.

The catchers moved in, but it was too early. The animal wasn't quite sedated. It lashed out with one of its strong legs and a web-clawed talon caught Joe's leg. His scream split the air. The crocodile had almost ripped the calf off Joe's bare leg; it was holding on by a third of its previous muscle and skin.

The men sprang into action to subdue the big crocodile, but that had been its last hurrah. Its eyes closed vertically and then fell back into their sockets, and the outer eyelids closed completely. The reptile slumped into the stillness of the comatose.

Spence ran to Joe, squeezed the torn calf muscle back together and applied as much pressure as he could to the slippery, bloody skin while the first-aid kit was retrieved and emergency services were called.

'All right, bring one of those croc stretchers here and we'll get Joe up to the road,' Spence said. 'It's easier and quicker than moving the croc, and I'm sure the ambos won't want to go anywhere near the croc, tranqed or not.'

Spence pointed to another catcher and called, 'You, go with Joe and call his family on the way.' Sorted, Spence thought. 'Now for this bloody reptile,' he said, with no love in his voice. 'Roll him off, fellas.'

They poked the beast with one of their long lasso poles first to test if the crocodile was totally out this time. There was an audible outlet of breath from the onlookers.

'One, two, roll,' said Spence.

It took four of the men to move the dead weight of the sleeping crocodile. It landed on its back with a thud, legs in the air. It was immediately apparent where the blood had come from. The crocodile's family jewels had been bitten off.

'Holy shit!' Spence said, almost inaudibly.

One of the catchers tasted the acrid taste of vomit on the back of his tongue, and there was nothing he could do to stop the contents of his stomach spraying over his shoes. A chain reaction of dry heaving followed, and most of the men, along with Ryan, unconsciously covered their own zippered area.

In the mouth of the victim was the penis of the large crocodile; it looked very similar to that of a male human. Two more men dry retched. Another, who was not as badly affected as the others, went to remove the appendage.

'Stop, leave the evidence,' McKay yelled as he slipped down the embankment.

'But we might be able to sew it back on,' the man called. 'It's a clean severing.'

'All right, but we need photos before you take it anywhere. And keep us informed about what happens with ...' McKay waved a hand vaguely towards the crocodile. He couldn't imagine life without his own penis and felt almost sorry for the man-eating reptile.

'I don't think there's much chance that this crime scene is going to be any use.' Ryan directed his statement at McKay.

'All good, I videoed the whole thing.' McKay held up his phone. 'We should be able to tell what area was compromised and what wasn't.'

'Forensics will still have to sieve the sand.' Ryan indicated the crime scene.

When the sleeping crocodile had been safely removed, the forensic pathologist, in her white disposable all-in-one coveralls, moved in and both detectives joined her.

'Caucasian, male, medium build, late thirties. By the look of it, he has a broken jaw.' She moved the jaw slightly side to side. 'And significant head trauma also.'

'Can you tell what could have caused the head trauma?' McKay leaned in.

'Mmm, something round, about the size of a twenty-cent piece.' She carefully pushed aside some of the victim's oily dark hair. 'Hard to tell until I get him in the shop and wash off some of these brain and skull particulars.' Scanning the rest of the victim's body, she added, 'I'll do up a full tox screen report and let you know what else I find. Bag him, fellas,' she said, like she said it every day.

The Bus Ride

It was not the first time Smithy had had to deal with someone from this particular group of bikies. Just last week a bikie from a chapter of well-known outlaw motorcycle gang, or OMG, had ridden along with the other shuttle-bus passengers from Cairns to Port Douglas. Why would a bikie take a shuttle bus, he wondered. And why the hell would he be travelling to Port Douglas? There wasn't much up there except lots of tourists and resorts. But Smithy had an inkling ...

The big burly bikie tossed a black overnight bag into the luggage section under the bus. I don't want to know, Smithy thought, I just have to drive them all there safely.

The shuttle bus was only a quarter full because a family of nine had cancelled half an hour before the bus was due to leave. Crap, the wages are going to be slim pickings again, Smithy thought. Luckily, he had a bit of extra cash coming in this week, even if it wasn't quite legit. You gotta do what you gotta do, he thought.

The bus ride to Port Douglas was scenic for the passengers. On the left was a tropical rainforest and on the right was Great Barrier Reef.

Smithy was on edge the whole trip, constantly looking in the rear-view mirror to keep an eye on the bikie, only to find dark eyes looking directly back into his own ocean-coloured eyes. Was he daft, or did the whites of the fella's eyes have a green tinge? Nah, geez, I've gotta lay off the grog, he thought.

The other passengers didn't seem to mind. They were too caught up in their holiday plans, or getting settled into their seats, to notice the bikie dressed in denim jeans and black T-shirt. Smithy knew, though. He had always wanted to be a detective. The look of those black bikie boots and the tat of a skull with wings that encompassed his arms gave it away.

Could this be the fella, Smithy wondered. He noticed that nobody sat next to the bikie. Smart people, he thought. If nobody pushed his buttons they'd have a nice, uneventful hour-and-a-half ride to Port Douglas.

Fifteen minutes later, the bus was quiet except for some chitter-chatter from the gap-year girls down the back. In Smithy's peripheral vision, he saw the bikie look over his shoulder. Crap, this could be trouble. The muscles in Smithy's back tightened, waiting for what was going to happen.

'Relax, old man, not my type,' the bikie said. 'They look like they'd bruise if I as much as looked at 'em.' He punched his own hand hard enough for the muscles to bunch up under his T-shirt.

Smithy slowly released the breath he'd been holding. Holy mother of … Smithy tried to swallow the heartbeat hammering in his throat. He thought about the flask of coffee with a dash in the small esky next to him. Christ, he could go a swig of that right about now.

'What's his problem?' said the tradie in his fluoro safety vest to nobody in particular, quietly enough that the giant behind the driver didn't hear him.

'I know, right?' replied the passenger in the seat in front of him. 'My job is stressful enough without thugs adding to it.'

The tradie reached between the seats and offered his calloused hand. 'Gary,' he said, his hand lingering in mid-air.

'Ian,' came the response finally.

Gary winced at the strong handshake from a guy who looked like to him like a typical bookworm. He pulled his hand back and gave it a rub. 'So, what do you do for a crust?'

'Wrestle crocs,' Ian said, and waited for the usual response.

'Seriously cool, mate.'

Mmm, I think I'm going to like this guy, Ian thought. 'Yeah, I get to play with hormones and scent, see what makes 'em tick.'

'You mean what makes 'em get it on?' Gary sniggered.

'That's right.' Ian ran a hand through his sun-bleached hair. 'But it can get a bit out of control if there are too many males around. The females are a bit bigger, but they can still get tossed around a bit and lose some of that leathery skin people like to make into handbags and belts.'

'I'd like to see that,' Gary said.

'Not if you were in the middle of collecting samples, you wouldn't.' Ian showed off a decent scar on his lower leg.

'Christ, mate, you're lucky you're here to tell the story.'

'I still think that when I pull my socks on.'

'So these scents, do you mean pheromones?' Gary mentally patted himself on the back for thinking of the word.

Ian's eyebrows rose in surprise. Mmm, he's a smart one, he thought. 'Nailed it.' He mimed the action of hammering a nail.

Gary lifted his own hammer from his toolbox and mimicked the same action. They both laughed.

The chatter and laughter from the back seat of the bus had slowly been getting louder.

A voice boomed from behind Smithy: 'Shut it, you lot!'

Smithy jumped in his seat. The voice had been right next to his ear, causing his head to spin and his vision go fuzzy. He was doing a hundred kilometres per hour when he lost control. The thirty-seater bus headed for the embankment, and the girls in the back of the bus screamed. A hand snaked around Smithy and took control of the steering wheel as he slumped back in the driver's seat. He didn't even notice the hand until his vision started to clear and the bus had slowed to a halt.

Passengers started to get up.

'*Sit the fuck down,*' boomed the bikie.

Everyone cowered and sat back down in their seats, terrified.

Ian stood up. 'Come on, mate,' he said to the bikie, 'we're all a bit antsy here. I think we all need a pee break and to stretch our legs.'

The bikie rolled his eyes. 'Get off, then.' He gestured angrily toward the doorway. When the passengers were slow to move, he boomed, *'Get off!'*

The girls squealed but started to file off more quickly, making sure not to make eye contact with the bikie.

'It's the middle of nowhere,' said the scientist, feeling brave enough to speak out. Some of the jelly was leaving his legs. 'Where are the girls going to pee?'

'I don't give a flying ... find a friggin' bush!' Anger rose in the bikie now, and the veins on the side of his head throbbed. Keep it cool, he told himself, keep it cool. Breathe. He had to get the cargo to Port Douglas with no one suspecting or the boss would skin him alive. He closed his eyes and drew in a deep breath. What a load of fucking crap, he thought. Deep breaths are bullshit. The blood pounded through his veins freely. A combination of the near crash and the racket from down the back set off his agitation in full force.

'Hey, it was only a question, no need to flip a gasket,' Ian said.

The bikie's teeth clenched and the muscles in his jaw rippled as he eyed the crocodile scientist. Fuck, he thought, I wanna pound him to a pulp.

His head screamed as the girls filed past him and the skirt of one of them grazed his arm. He grabbed the young blonde's buttock and squeezed hard, making her cry out. He laughed. 'You wanna bit of this?' He grabbed his crotch and rubbed the rising mound in his jeans. The terror in her eyes only egged him on. 'Come on, sweetheart, I bet you've never had something as hard as this sliding up your thigh.'

The girl gagged as she tried to pull away. The anger he regarded as a close friend rose to a new level, and he grabbed her by the hair and pushed her across the seats, face down. Her skirt was short; the G-string that didn't hide a lot just fuelled his lust.

'Now, there's a pussy I'd like to play with, little girl.' He held her down with one hand in the middle of her back, and reached for his zip with the other and lowered it quickly. 'This'll be quick.' He laughed, eyes on the squirming girl in front of him. 'Keep still, you little whor—'

Before he could finish his sentence he began to jerk uncontrollably. A small amount of green froth dribbled from his mouth, unseen by the others. It was quick. Brain matter splashed the seats around him. A chunk of skull was caught in the girl's hair, and she squealed, desperately trying to get it out but it became even more entangled.

The bikie was silent now. His elbow collapsed under his dead weight and he fell forward, squashing the girl underneath him. His genitals were crammed up hard against her unprotected nether regions and her squirming only made the situation worse. Her screams were renewed as sticky fluid dribbled down her legs.

'Get him off! Get him *off*!' she screamed. 'He's coming, get him *off*!'

The bikie was yanked backwards by the green leather belt of his jeans, his member still dripping its fluids.

The girl, now free, twisted and rolled to the floor between the seats and landed with a thud. She sat up and bawled at the sight of the partially undressed bikie so close to her face, but when she looked up she was shocked into silence as shards of his skull and brain matter slid down his cheek. The bus was silent except for the girl's snivelling.

Ian was still holding the hammer aloft. Stunned, he lowered it slowly.

Smithy, now recovered from his vision loss, gently pried it from Ian's unresponsive hand. It had all been so quick that Smithy hadn't even seen the scientist take the hammer from the tradie's toolbox.

Forensics

'No ID on the John Doe?' said the chief medical examiner, or Doc Carol, as she was known in the field.

'None we could find. Did you have any more luck than us, doc?' said Ryan.

'Not yet,' she said, getting on with the reason she'd brought the detectives in. 'The obvious cause of death would be the 29-millimetre-diameter hole in the back of the vic's head, but I don't think that's what killed him.'

The detectives glanced at each other. 'So, what are you thinking?' Ryan said, walking closer to the corpse.

'Some sort of poisoning,' she said.

'Any clues to what it is?'

'Some. The whites of his eyes and fingernails have a green tinge, and I found green foam inside his mouth, along with reptile semen,' she said, glossing over the fact that this didn't happen every day, and continued before the detectives could ask the burning question she knew they wanted answered. 'On dissecting the vic's liver and lungs, I discovered the exact same green tinge.'

'What about this green line around his waist?' Ryan moved closer. 'I feel like I've seen something like this before,' he said, touching the line with a gloved hand, 'and it doesn't rub off.'

'Correct. It looks like it's been there for a while. I believe it's from his belt. Late eighteen hundreds, I suspect, going on the brass buckle.'

'Crikey, it should be in a museum,' said McKay.

'I've sent off samples of the leather and buckle for testing. Results should be back later today,' said the doctor, seeing the query on McKay's face. 'I put a rush on it in case we need to inform the infectious diseases department.'

'Should we be wearing masks?' McKay said.

'No, or I would be.'

Relief flooded McKay's face.

'Photos of his tattoos have also been sent off for verification.' She indicated the markings on his neck and arms. 'The tattoo register should pick up something before the facial-recognition program finishes.'

Diiinnnggg.

'That's the results now.' She walked over to the computer for a closer look. Her eyebrows arched. 'By these results, we have a Mr King, a Mr Wayne King.' She turned to see Ryan stroking the corpse's forearm in a daze. 'What the hell are you doing?'

McKay smirked.

Ryan snatched his hand away. 'Um, I have no idea why I did that.'

The coroner pistol-gripped her chin, thinking, 'Okay, this might sound totally insignificant but ...' She turned to Ryan and McKay. 'I did exactly the same thing not half an hour ago.'

'You stand next to him, McKay.' Ryan hoped like hell it would happen to his partner.

McKay did as he was asked. Nothing. But he did sneeze.

The brain block dropped quickly from the coroner's mind. She snapped her fingers. 'Pheromones, it has to be pheromones. That would explain the semen in the vic's mouth. It would have to be a very strong copulin-oxytocin mix, though.' She rubbed her hands in thought.

Ryan cringed. 'You should've heard it when the jaw cracked. The noise is impaled in my memory forever. Here, I have it on vid—'

'I'll watch it later. Is it on file?'

'Sure is, under John Doe 396, which I will change as soon as I get back to my desk,' said McKay. 'What was his name again? Ah, Wayne King,' and sniggered at the name.

'I'm glad he was dead before that happened.' Ryan rubbed the corpse's arm again and snatched his hand away, hoping nobody saw him.

'Me, too,' said the coroner in a matter-of-fact way, 'or we would've lost vital evidence.'

She moved the industrial-strength magnifying glass over the corpse's neck. She could see small amounts of residue she'd previously thought of as dried seawater. She'd taken a sample and sent it off to the lab, but the results had not come back yet. 'It wasn't long after I took the samples that I found myself mindlessly stroking the vic myself.'

A barely stifled guffaw broke the silence.

'Farrrk,' said Ryan, 'I was getting it on with a corpse.'

McKay couldn't hold it in any longer. He laughed so hard tears streamed down his checks.

'All right, all right, this goes no further than this room.' Ryan looked directly at McKay.

McKay held up his hands in submission and nodded, unable to speak yet. He drew in a deep breath and said, 'This is absolute *gold*,' and laughed all over again.

Ryan knew Doc Carol wouldn't say anything because she'd done exactly the same thing, but McKay ... He could see it now, one drunken afternoon at the local and it would be out. 'Ah, stuff it.'

The Bikies

Smithy hummed part of the chorus to his favourite song — *oh lar la lar liddy dar* — while he prepared the shuttle bus for the next load of passengers.

'Geezuz h — you scared the living daylights out of me.' He turned quickly, sensing that somebody was behind him. Wrong move, he thought, lowering his eyes to see the man's clenched fist. He read the single letter tattooed on the three fingers he could see: *HEL* …

Smithy's eyes twitched, wanting to pop from their sockets, but as he raised his eyes he knew he had to keep it cool and put on his best poker face. Standing mere inches from his nose was one of ugliest bikies he'd ever laid eyes on. The stench Smithy inhaled was a mix of old ashtray, rancid alcohol and the smell of something he couldn't quite put his finger on. To him, it smelled like death.

None of that mattered, though. It was going down, and he was in the middle of it without even trying. Why does trouble always seem to follow me, he thought. His shoulders slumped.

'Come on, mate, we just wanna get a look inside.' The bikie pointed to the cargo hull of the shuttle bus.

'I'd love to oblige you, but I've got a bus load of passengers coming any moment,' Smithy fibbed, and hoped it was his best ever. He knew the passengers weren't due for another hour, but that's all that popped into his head.

Smithy saw the bikie look around the parking lot of the hotel, seeing nobody. His heart skipped a beat. The bikie reached for Smithy's shoulder and squeezed hard until the pain became too much.

'I'm trying to make this easy on ya, mate,' the bikie said. 'Just give it up and we'll be on our way. You know the deal.' He squeezed harder. 'We've got a funeral to go to.'

Smithy wondered how much the bikies could possibly know. His heartbeat had risen and dark spots danced in his eyes. He knew the black bag was still in the cargo hull, and he hoped like hell they wouldn't feel any weight difference.

Geez, he thought, imagine lining up around the coffin of that friggin' lunatic as it was being lowered. No friggin' way. As far as Smithy was concerned, that scumbag got what he deserved and then some. He thought back to the recent television reports. How could he have known the idiot bikie passenger had been newly patched?

Smithy pictured himself grabbing the unusual green belt of the dead bikie, and sliding the dead weight of the body down the embankment to the secluded beach not far from where the bus had crashed. He also remembered clearly what the crocodile scientist had said.

Those pheromones will do the trick.

Well, that was the so-called stinking good plan they'd come up with. Now he knew it was just stinking; there was no good about it.

Seeing the body on the news in the pub the night before had rocked his world completely. His hand had shot out to grab the bar, and he'd automatically asked for a shot. He downed it quickly. It wasn't the time to finally go on the wagon. Two or three shots later, and the blood was no longer trying to burst through his veins. Geezuz. He'd been waiting for the cops to burst through his front door at home, slap cuffs on him and read him his rights, but this was another kettle of fish.

The news report mentioned a thirty-five-year-old male known as Wayne King. Smithy had sniggered. Wish I'd known that last week, he thought. Wayne King had been found on a secluded beach between Cairns and Port Douglas. If anyone had information regarding this man's death they were asked to call the Crime Stoppers number. A photo of the man had been shown on screen for a few seconds.

Smithy ran his plump hand through his greying hair. Everybody on the bus had exchanged contact details via business cards except the for gap-year girls; their numbers were written on purple paper that smelt like lavender. The contact numbers were all still in his wallet and he knew he should get rid of them. How would he explain the addresses to the cops?

'Off with the friggin' fairies,' said the bikie to the other chapter members who'd arrived behind him. 'This guy is a loon or wants to be dead.' The bikie reapplied the earlier Vulcan grip to Smithy's shoulder and it finally pulled him out of his trance. 'Give me the bag,' he said.

It's not worth my life, Smithy thought, but subconsciously he knew it very well could be. He leaned down and unlatched the cargo hull. 'You said I could go free, right? That it was a one-off.'

'Sorry, mate. You took your sweet-arse time answering me and now you're coming with us until we check the contents. You'd better hope it's all there.'

'But my passengers—'

'Stuff your passengers.'

Smithy was dragged to a souped-up Ford Mustang and shoved in.

'We're off to a funeral,' the bikie said.

When they finally arrived at their destination, Smithy wasn't sure if he'd make it through this. He stood in the circle of the outlaw motorcycle gang, or one-percenters, as they were also known, while the casket was lowered into the ground. He tried to hide his face, but it was useless. News cameras were everywhere.

The large OMG bikie looked up and there was an instant moment of silence. Then *click-click-click*.

They're game, Smithy thought, looking at the photographers. He looked into the crowd and hoped someone could see he wasn't there by choice. Beads of sweat glistened on his forehead. This was the closest he'd ever felt to death. *Come on; let's get it done already.* He hadn't felt this uncomfortable since the birth of his first child in the back of the family stationwagon, back before there were mobile phones, and he had been sweating bullets then.

The president of the OMG knelt down, grabbed a handful of dirt and threw it on the casket. The sergeant at arms knelt down to copy the president, and the black bag taunted Smithy as it swung from two fingers. This was the sign for all the other chapter members to follow suit. Smithy waited until they had all paid their respects and did exactly the same, but added a small parcel along with the dirt. Luckily for him, the amount of dirt already on the coffin muffled the sound of his wallet hitting the casket. He threw down his own handful of dirt to cover it.

Finally, he thought, a lucky break. Even if he got through this, which he knew he had Buckley's chance of doing, he thought it'd been a genius move to erase his wallet from existence. At least the business cards and lavender notes would be gone.

The sergeant at arms turned just in time to see Smithy straighten up. 'Nice touch, paying your respects, but it's not going to help you if it's not all here,' he said, swinging the black bag back and forth.

Smithy stared back with his best poker face and said nothing. Finally breaking the man's gaze, he looked around. There would be no getting past the paparazzi without his face ending up on tonight's news. So he held his head up high and walked straight through the barricade of cameras. *Click-click-click.* He hoped they got his good side, at least.

Once again he found himself pushed unceremoniously into the metallic Mustang. On any other day he would have liked to run his hand over the meticulous paintwork that changed from maroon to gold, depending on where you stood. It's a thing of beauty, he thought wistfully.

The drive was silent and Smithy was fine with that.

'All right,' said the gravelly voice beside him.

Smithy physically jumped in his seat, turned and gawked at the speaker. 'Ah, yes.'

'We know he was only just patched and initiated, but how the hell did he end up on the beach dead?'

Explanations

'It was all fine until the bus had an accident and then the shit hit the fan.' Smithy turned away for a moment, remembering. 'There were bits of brain everywhere.' He squirmed in his seat. 'The young blood snapped a brain cell and tried to rape one of the passengers, and the others retaliated with a hammer to the noggin.'

The president looked hard and long at Smithy until the other man squirmed again.

'Geezuz, the whole situation was out of control. The drop would've been compromised with the cops crawling all over the bus,' Smithy said, looking straight ahead. 'So here it is. This is not what I thought being on the take would be. Things got out of hand way too quick and there was nothing I could do. I want out.' He knew his words were lost on them. They didn't care; they just wanted their cash and stash.

Beside him, the sergeant at arms unzipped the bag tediously slowly. Smithy could hear each zip tooth releasing.

'Well, you're in luck,' said the president, and Smithy's head snapped around. 'I have intel on the feds. They say he died from arsenic poisoning.'

'What?' Smithy looked dumbfounded.

'They say the green belt was the cause of death. That girl's lucky he didn't do the deed or she would've been poisoned as well.'

'Geezuz, I touched it.'

'From what I heard, it takes years for the toxic levels to build up enough to kill you.'

'But the girl ...'

'He had enough in his bloodstream and semen to affect her.'

'That would account for the weird jerking he did.' Smithy wiped a hand across his forehead. 'I thought it was just some new technique the young 'uns did these days.'

'He was well and truly fucked long before that,' the president said. 'It was lucky he'd lasted that long.'

The other man sniggered and the zipper noise stopped. 'Yeah, the croc was giving it to him, and because you left him clothed the croc used his mouth.'

A gagging sound came from beside him. Smithy was glad he hadn't eaten. 'Oh, geezuz, no wonder the body was found still on the beach. The scientist had promised it'd work.' Had the scientist known all along what was going to happen? Was it his friggin' payback for the girl's situation, a do-unto-others type thing?

The group on the bus had made a pact: no talking about what had happened, *ever*. Smithy was able to clean the bus of any evidence and restarted it without too much effort, thankful to the bikie now for taking the wheel. There was no exterior damage to the bus, and at the time he'd been sure they would get away with it.

The zip continued faster now. Knuckles, the sergeant at arms, handed the bag to President Widowmaker without even sneaking a peek.

'What the ...'

The reaction wasn't a shock to Smithy. He'd known exactly what wasn't in the bag, but when the cold metal of the pistol was pressed against his head an involuntary gush of blood swam violently through his body, causing his head to spin. What would they do if I passed out, he thought. And then he did just that.

They had stopped; the rocks that dug into Smithy's back told him he was no longer in the car.

'For fuck's sake, mate, you know it's gonna happen, take it like a man,' said Knuckles, shaking him none too gently.

Smithy hadn't regained consciousness properly when he smelled gunpowder and heard a safety being released. It was quick. A flash of light and Smithy ceased to exist.

His body was found on the side of the road. The one-percenters were seriously pissed but felt justified with the death. After all, somebody had to pay for their fallen kinsman. Hell, they couldn't tell the chapter it was the stupid belt that had killed their newest member, and besides, the money and stash had been taken. It's retribution, they reasoned. They'd have to rethink who they used next time. No more newly patched jokers. Just put one of their own at the wheel of the bus. Why hadn't they thought of it before?

'Christ,' said the president, 'I'm gonna clang heads for this.'

The Stash

The girls ended up having a rad time in Port Douglas with all the extra cash Smithy had shared around, but the drugs were fed to the crashing waves. No way were they going to get caught with that stash. There was some commotion at the time about keeping samples, but Smithy was adamant that it *all* had to go. He might have been a drunk, but he had morals. No loose ends for the cops to find, he'd thought at the time.

It was a shock when they'd seen Smithy's death on the news only days after the report on the dead bikie. The news reporter had said: 'The bus driver, Mr Paul Smith, has been linked with a well-known outlaw motorcycle gang, and was seen at the recent funeral of one of their chapter members. But it is reported that Paul Smith's death is suspicious and possibly gang related.'

Did he squeal, the remaining bus passengers wondered. Would the bikies come for them next? This unanswered question kept them all on edge for many years after the incident.

Archives

Detective Sergeant McKay slid the archive box onto the shelf in the case warehouse. On the box was written CLOSED and KING W. There was no way the police could have found any evidence on the beach after the fiasco of catching the crocodile. They didn't push it, either. They knew the reason for Wayne King's death was the arsenic that seeped from his vintage belt and not the head wound.

'Did we ever find out why King wore that green belt?' Ryan leaned against a nearby archive box.

'I did a bit of digging, and it turns out it was a family heirloom from three generations.' McKay took out his phone to show his partner what he'd found. 'Looking at his father's, grandfather's and great-grandfather's death certificates, it shows they all died due to convulsions that were diagnosed as epileptic fits.'

'Farrrk, you're telling me they all wore that death trap of a belt?'

'Yes, I suspect they all died of arsenic poisoning,' said McKay.

'What a way to cull a family line.'

'According to his father's rap sheet, he was a member of the same bikie chapter as his son.'

'The apple doesn't fall far from the tree.' Ryan lifted the bagged green belt from the archive box he'd slid back out. 'There are just some things you don't want to hand down to your son, and this is a prime example.' He snapped open the ziplock bag and that faraway look crossed his face again.

McKay recognised that faraway look on his partner's face again. He laughed, remembering the scene at the coroner's office, and took out his phone to photograph Ryan in his state of stupor. Here we go again, he thought.

The Brisbane Strangler

Chris Childs

t was one of those deliciously balmy Brisbane evenings. The October sky was clear. Moonlight danced merrily on the river's surface.

The party was rocking to the 1985 top forty when, overwhelmed by strangers shouting inane greetings across a roomful of gyrating dancers, I escaped outside for some fresh air and solitude. I strolled to the bottom of the garden, where a jacaranda was in full bloom and the cicadas were screaming louder than Bruce Springsteen.

I hadn't been to a party in ages. After Mike and I had parted company three years ago—due to his terminal penchant for bleached blondes—I'd become a bit of a hermit. My usual Saturday-night activity was a toasted cheese sandwich and murder mysteries on TV. I loved shows about crime. I didn't care whether they were fact or fiction, although I confess to a weakness for corny American detective series.

My latest hobby was closer to home. Three young women had been strangled within the metropolitan area in the past few months. The police could find nothing concrete to connect the women other than their hair colour, and they had all met their fate by strangulation, in suburbs close to the Brisbane River.

Following the media coverage had become an obsession. My best friend, Helen, said I was a sad case who needed to get out and meet people. She meant guys, of course. So here I was at her party in her riverside Queenslander. I'd only agreed to come to get her off my back for a while.

I checked my watch for the tenth time and wondered when I could leave the party without offending her. Damn. Nine-thirty. Best put in another appearance inside and look like I'm making an effort, I thought reluctantly. I developed a plan to do a complete circumnavigation of the interior of the house, ensuring that I talked to at least three people in Helen's line of sight before making a hasty retreat.

A gentle cough startled me. I realised with a shock that I wasn't alone. I recognised Helen's friend, Tom, as he stepped under the porch light, clutching a nearly empty bottle of Asti spumante. He was hard to miss in his bright orange Hawaiian shirt and early-season tan.

'Tom's got a yacht,' Helen had said at the beginning of the evening, pushing us towards each other. 'Jean's into sailing, too,' she'd lied, desperately searching for some connection between us when there likely wasn't one.

It didn't work, and I escaped to the toilet after five minutes of uncomfortable small talk.

'I believe from Helen that we share a common interest,' Tom slurred as I reluctantly approached the porch.

Helen's been ad-libbing again, I thought with dismay, unless it's still the sailing thing.

'I hear you're a crime fan,' Tom said, persevering.

I groaned inwardly. Everyone's an amateur sleuth or psychologist. Still, I had to give Tom top marks for trying. It made a change from the usual testosterone-driven drivel guys usually spouted when they first met me.

'So, what's your theory about the strangler? Suppressed homosexual or mother hater?' he continued.

I couldn't decide if Tom was a kindred spirit, or a drunken weirdo to be avoided at all costs. I decided to give him the benefit of the doubt, but felt that the strangler was too dangerous a topic. I attempted to distract him with a critical analysis of the latest episode of *Columbo*. Fortunately it worked.

'Fancy a walk along the river?' Tom asked later, when we'd exhausted all of our favourite TV crime shows of the 60s and 70s, and up to the present-day 80s. 'I need to check that no one's stolen my boat.'

What could be the harm in that, I thought.

We walked in silence along the bank of the Brisbane River, both temporarily lost in our own thoughts.

'There she is,' Tom said proudly, pointing to a white cabin cruiser anchored about five metres from the river's edge.

'How do you get out there?' My voice came out in a nervous squeak.

I half hoped he wouldn't invite me on board. I didn't like to feel out of my depth, literally or physically. I couldn't swim more than a few doggy-paddle strokes. Besides, I had on a new Vanessa Richmond dress that I'd bought from the Riverside markets. I was pretty sure river water and pure silk wouldn't be a good mix.

He gestured towards a small metal dingy tied to a post on the jetty with a weather-beaten rope. Then he grabbed the rope and said, 'Hop in.'

I hesitated.

'Don't worry, I'm not the strangler, and even if I were, you're safe, he doesn't do brunettes,' he said, laughing at his own pathetic joke.

I realised that the fine hairs on the back of my neck were standing on end and my arms had broken out in goosebumps. All my usual warning signs were engaged. I wondered if anyone from the party had seen us leave together. I thought not. No one knew where we were, or that we were together. Anything could happen. I wondered if I should I walk away before any harm was done.

What the hell, I thought, making a snap decision against my better judgment. I reminded myself that I was physically stronger than I looked, and much more sober than Tom.

I accepted his outstretched hand and stepped into the dinghy with a growing sense of excitement. Maybe the evening wasn't going to be a disappointment after all.

The following morning I poured myself a cup of tea and switched on the TV for the latest news. There was a live cross to a local reporter, who was standing on the banks of the Brisbane River. The camera showed the Breakfast Creek Hotel in the distance before zooming in on an object floating in the river.

A body, face down, bobbed in the gently lapping waves, a bright orange shirt fanning out on top of the water like a butterfly's wings.

I made a mental note to get a copy of the *Courier-Mail* for my scrapbook, then turned off the TV and got ready for work.

The One That Didn't Get Away

Lea Scott

'**Y**ou shoulda seen the size of 'er!' Fred stretched his arms out as far as they would reach. 'She's a beauty, I tell you. I almost had 'er in the boat this time, but right at the last minute the damn line snapped and she swam off into the deep blue yonder.'

Matt chuckled and shook his head. 'That's a real bummer, Uncle Fred.'

All Matt's life, Fred had told him stories of the one that got away. Whenever he returned from one of his solitary fishing trips on the river, he told the story of the same big Murray cod that had been eluding him for years. Each year the cod and its legend grew bigger. Matt used to be in awe of the story when he was younger, but he now knew that the tales were as tall as his uncle, who often stooped to mask his six-foot-four stature.

'I know, I know,' Matt finished the story, 'one day you're gonna land that big one.' His eyes mocked Fred across the counter.

Fred swiped a hand in Matt's direction, but Matt knew there was no intention for it to land. He dropped his head and sipped from his straw until a loud gurgle rose from his milkshake.

The tinkle of the alert bell on the door shook Fred from his reverie as he looked up to see who might be entering his cafe so late in the evening. It was almost nine and he was about to close up shop for the night.

A woman in a hooded coat stepped through the doorway, ushering an adolescent girl into the warm room. The woman removed her hood. Fred felt his knees weaken as a feeling of recognition swept over him. Was it really her, after all these years?

She was older, but her eyes still held the softness of youth. She looked just how he imagined she would. His fingers touched his parted lips. Would she recognise him? He knew that time had not been as kind to him. His chest tightened as she neared the counter. He ran a hand over his stiff grey hair, conscious that it needed cutting.

Matt lifted his head from his drink. 'Are you okay, Uncle Fred? You look like you just saw a ghost.'

Fred nodded his head without taking his eyes from the woman's face.

Matt turned to follow his uncle's gaze. 'Who's she?' he whispered.

'Mary,' Fred whispered back, his voice trailing off as she stepped in front of him.

Her smile was warm and just as bright as he remembered. Fred found himself smiling back like an eager puppy, but his tongue felt numb, and he feared it might slide out of the corner of his mouth and embarrass him. He tried to greet her like any new customer, but the words caught in his throat. He saw the glimmer of recognition in her eyes, and in that moment he wished the ground would open up and swallow him.

'Fred?'

'H-hello, Mary.' There was a slight quiver in his voice.

She didn't seem to notice. 'Wow, you're still here, after all these years.'

'Sure am.' He forced a smile to his face.

'Do you and your wife run this place now?'

Fred felt warmth creep into his cheek. 'Never married.' He looked down at the counter. The only woman he had ever wanted to marry stood in front of him. The problem was that he had never been brave enough to tell her, or even to ask her out.

Mary stepped aside to reveal the young girl hiding behind her. 'This is my daughter, Freya.'

Fred noticed the girl steal a coy look at his nephew before she said, in a polite tone, 'Hello, nice to meet you.'

Freya had the same doe-brown eyes as her mother. Mary's eyes had mesmerised him twenty years ago, and the recollection transported him back to their first meeting.

He had been a shy teenager then, just short of his eighteenth birthday. She was the cousin of his best friend, visiting for the school holidays. The three of them had spent the entire summer swimming in the local creek and exploring the thick scrub surrounding the town. Fred had taught Mary how to fish in the river, baiting the hook for her and guiding her arms from behind as she learned to cast the line. He remembered the warmth of her body when she was close to him, and the blush returned to his cheek.

He handed a menu over the counter, hiding his emotions behind it. 'Please, pull up a pew. I'll be with you in just a tic.'

As he watched her walk to a nearby table, the doorbell sounded again. A smartly dressed man entered the cafe. He looked briefly around the room then headed toward the table where Mary and her daughter had just taken a seat.

Fred noticed the man's greying hair but otherwise trim appearance. He looked down on his own spreading paunch and sucked it in a little.

The man stooped down and kissed Mary and Freya on the top of the head before taking a seat opposite them.

Who is he, Fred wondered. This wasn't part of the plan.

Fred couldn't help but feel a stab of jealousy. Caring for his ailing mother for the past thirty years had robbed him of any chance of a social life, or of forming solid relationships. How different his life might have been if he'd only had the courage to tell Mary how he felt all those years ago. Would he still be in this small town, serving the same people every day?

It wasn't that he didn't enjoy his chosen vocation. Being part of the lives of people he knew well brought him a sense of contentment. But he had always felt there was something he had missed out on in life. Now here it was, slapping him in the face as he watched the happy family chatting across the table.

He turned to Matt, who was making eyes at the girl across the room. 'You think you could take their order?'

'You betcha,' Matt said, as he jumped off the chair, eager to have a reason to talk to the attractive young girl.

'Cheers, I'll be in the kitchen.' Fred pushed his way through the swinging doors and then stood with his back against the wall, trying not to tremble as he drew in the smell of fresh bread and cooking oil. He tried to let the familiar scent of his kitchen occupy his senses until he had calmed a little.

Fred had tried his best, which, as usual, wasn't good enough. If his mother had still been here, she would have said, 'Try harder.' He felt his fist bunch, and hid it under his apron.

Matt entered the kitchen with the order, and Fred busied himself preparing the meals. He took care to make a colourful arrangement of edible flowers on top of Mary's salad. He had introduced the speciality to the cafe after reading about it in a glossy food magazine. He grew the flowers himself in a climate-controlled greenhouse in his back garden, and was especially proud of the fact that he had been able to nurture varieties that would not normally grow here in the cold.

After sending Matt back out to deliver the food, Fred remained in the kitchen, cleaning and tidying up. He couldn't face Mary. Not now that he knew the risks he had taken had been wasted and she would never be his.

Sometime later, the swinging doors opened and he glanced up to see Matt grinning at him. 'Mary wants to say goodbye.' He winked.

Fred shook his head, but Matt pushed him through the doors. He took hesitant steps toward the counter, where Mary stood waiting.

'I wanted to say goodbye,' she said, with a broad smile. 'It was so good to see you, and thank you for the wonderful meal. We've travelled a long way tonight.'

Fred felt stupid for not passing on his condolences. 'Oh, of course, you're here for the funeral.' Mary's aunt, his best friend's mother, had been found dead on the floor of her bedroom earlier in the week. 'I was so sorry to hear about your aunt.'

'I was sorry to hear about your mother's recent passing, too,' she said in the sincerest tone. 'Will I see you there? At the funeral?'

Fred looked down at his outstretched hands on the counter and muttered, 'Not very good at funerals.'

Mary's voice became a conspiratorial whisper, although there was nobody in earshot. 'You know they say she was poisoned. Maybe even murdered.'

Fred nodded, with his eyes still averted.

'Yes, I suppose you knew that. I forgot that everyone knows everyone and everything that goes on in this town.' Her eyes moistened. 'I just can't understand who would want to do that to such a sweet old lady. Or why.'

Fred was unable to respond. When he dared to look back up, the pain in her eyes was almost his undoing.

'I'm sorry. I didn't mean to lay all this on you.' She brushed her smooth fingers over his. 'Well, it was nice to see you, anyway. You take care.'

Fred pulled his fingers away, afraid that his trembling hand might give him away. He turned in an attempt to retreat to the safety of his kitchen.

'By the way,' she called out, forcing him to turn back, 'did you ever read that fishing book I gave you?'

He thought back to the last day he had seen her that summer. It had been the day of his eighteenth birthday. She had presented him with a beautiful hardcover book on salmon fishing in exotic locations. When would he ever have had the chance to leave his small town and go to places like that? It was a nice gesture, but he had put it on his bookshelf and not given it another thought.

'No,' he said, his feet shuffling. 'I never did get the time to read it.'

'Oh. I guess that explains it, then.' Her smile turned somewhat awkward as she spun around and headed out the door.

The man and the young girl were making their way out of the cafe.

'Come on, Grandad, you slowcoach,' Fred heard the girl call out.

Grandad? He was such an idiot. The man must have been the father of Mary's late husband. Fred wanted to run out the door after her, but his feet were rooted to the ground. Still, his plan was not a total washout. Perhaps he would go to the funeral after all.

Later that evening, Fred pulled the fishing book from his shelf. He had been heartbroken when she left, so it had sat there unread for twenty years. He ran his hand over the thick and pristine pages. They didn't make books of this quality anymore. He had only plucked it of the shelf last weekend and discovered it's long-held secret. He flicked through the book, stopping to take in some of the glossy picture plates of smiling men holding giant salmon in their arms.

As he turned the pages, a small piece of folded paper fell to the floor. He stooped to pick it up and smiled at the heart drawn on the front in thick red felt pen. Inside the heart, his initials had been written: FV.

His heart hammered in his chest, even though he had read the note many times during the week. He unfolded the paper, his clumsy fingers trembling. Inside, the writing was pink. He heard Mary's lyrical young voice in his head as he read the words she had written the day before she walked out of his life: Meet me at our place by the river tomorrow at lunchtime. It was signed xxx.

His eyes crinkled as he stared at the note. A tear rolled down his cheek, falling and landing on the inked heart, which began to spread in a red blot across the paper. All these years he had been telling his nephew the story of the one that got away from his fishing line, but the real one he had hooked and let slip from his grasp was Mary.

When he had found the note last week, he knew it was a sign. He had driven to the library and asked the librarian to help him look up Mary's whereabouts. He'd heard about that Facebook thing from Matt and hoped she had an account. He found her, and spent hours working his way back through her timeline until he found the funeral notice for her late husband two years prior.

He was certain that finding her note was a sign that they were meant to reunite.

He had tried to write her a letter, but each time he began, he didn't know what to say and ended up screwing the paper, with his few futile words, into a ball and throwing it into the kitchen bin. And then he would stare at the overflowing bin, hearing his mother's voice in his head telling him he should take out the rubbish.

It was during such a moment that he had conceived his plan to bring Mary back to town. He knew how close she had been to her aunt.

The elderly librarian hadn't suspected a thing. He doubted she would ever mention it to the police. Even if she remembered him making enquiries about Mary, it was a long stretch to connect him to her aunt's death. The plant was still a problem, though. He picked up the local newspaper and perused the story again.

According to the article, a glycosoide poison called oleandrin was the culprit that had poisoned Mary's aunt. It came from the oleander, a plant that didn't grow very well in the cold region where the town was situated, so the police had concluded that it was unlikely she had come into contact with it naturally. They suspected foul play, but they could not come up with any feasible motive for the murder of the long-term elderly resident, or a likely suspect. Her home and her financial affairs were all in order.

Fred put the paper down. They never would work it out if he had anything to do with it.

Fred's mother had been ill for so long that her doctor hadn't requested an autopsy when he pronounced her dead in her bed one chilly morning last month. Fred hadn't been so fortunate with Mary's aunt. She had loved the salads he delivered to her, adorned with lovely colourful flowers. It had not been too hard for him to add a few oleander leaves and flowers to her daily meal. He knew that it would be quick, given her already poor health.

He peered through the window at the steam rising from his climate-controlled greenhouse. He pulled his coat from the hook on the back of the door and headed out into the garden. He plucked his beloved oleander plant from the shelf in the greenhouse and stroked the soft pink flowers. It would be a shame to lose it from his collection, but it had served him well.

He pulled the plant from its pot and ran it through his electric leaf mulcher until it was nothing more than shreds of compost material. He gathered up all the material carefully and spread it around the new garden bed he had dug by the back fence. The toxin in the leaves would deteriorate within about fifty days and leave no trace of the murder weapon the police sought.

Fred scrubbed his hands with strong soap to remove the poison. He headed back inside to spruce up his appearance. He had been a dutiful son, caring for his mother and abiding by her final wish to end her suffering when the doctors had refused. One big bowl of oleander soup, a few of her strong painkillers to ease any discomfort, and it was all over.

It would only have been a matter of time before Mary's terminally ill aunt would have asked the same of him. He had done her the kindest of favours, and she had returned it by bringing Mary back to him so he could recapture her heart.

He turned off the hair clippers. He noticed a stray hair in his nostril and plucked it away with his big fingers. It was time to work out what he would wear to the funeral tomorrow to impress Mary.

Killer Bait

Diane K Edwards

'It's happened again, sir.' Detective Sergeant Sandra studied her boss, who was sitting high in his worn, grey leather office chair, with his do-not-disturb-unless-really-really-important demeanour. Well, this *was* important because it had happened again.

'Go on then, Willoughby, spit it out.'

Detective Inspector John Reeves was feeling impatient beyond belief. He hadn't had an enviable day, what with the superintendent's visit and the budget cut that ensued. Plus, there were other aggravating incidents, like his boss reminding him of the discussion they'd had a month ago. John Reeves let his mind wander back there.

'John,' the superintendent had said solemnly, 'I'm sorry, but you have to be replaced. Sandra Willoughby's going to step into your role. She dresses smartly and is well educated. She's ideal for the role of head of investigations. She's a hard worker, that one, and we want her in your seat. It's time to retire, John. It's time you stepped aside for a young and powerful woman who runs rings around you. You've got a month, and then we're offering her the role.'

Sandra started again. 'Well, sir, there's been another incident, another fatality.'

Three times in the last month, young women had been assaulted on their way home from work. The first victim had been bashed with a weighty object and strangled. Not pretty, and she was very, very dead.

The second woman, just days later, had lived through the ordeal of attempted strangulation but was in a coma and not expected to pull through. It would be some time before she could be interviewed, if at all.

The third victim was found three weeks later on the same path, the one that led from the train to the station car park.

Despite hours of police work interviewing and scrutinising all the people on the trains before, during and after the discoveries, and searching the bushes and car park for clues, plus looking through hours of CCTV footage, so far there had been no concrete leads.

One common factor in all the attacks was that none of the girls had been sexually assaulted. Considering the severity of the crimes and the profile of the victims, it was very strange indeed. Uncovering a motive would be difficult.

Sandra stared intently at her boss's furrowed brow. She wondered if he was even interested in what she had to say. She tried again. 'I'm sorry, sir, it's just that it's happened again, in the same place.'

John Reeves looked up from the chip in the desk that he had been studying and tried to show interest in what his detective was saying. 'Okay,' he said gruffly. 'Details?'

Sandra thought it strange that a man of his standing should have so few words at a time like this. Surely he should show more interest, or at least feign interest, for the sake of the victims. She was getting a tad frustrated. It's time John Reeves took a step back, she thought.

'Eighteen-year-old girl, Caucasian, wearing office clothes, dead,' she said. 'Struck with a weighty object and then strangled. Estimated time of death, six-thirty last night. The body was found in the bushes this morning by a jogger—'

'And?' John Reeves once again lifted his eyes from his desk to stare directly into Sandra's own wide eyes.

Geez, thought Sandra, give me a minute to finish. 'CCTV footage shows the woman leaving the train at six twenty-five pm and heading down a partially obscured path to the car park. No sign of her emerging from the path at the other end.'

She stopped and searched her boss's eyes for a sign of incredulousness. After all, it was obvious that the woman would not have been seen at the other end of the path because she was dead before she got there.

But he said nothing.

'No witnesses at all,' she continued. 'I interviewed all the commuters and train staff, also door-knocked in the vicinity, but no luck yet.'

'How bad are her injuries?' John felt it was important to ask about the injuries the woman had sustained. He wanted to appear to be establishing plausible motives for the murders. They weren't sexually driven, so what could be the reason behind these heinous crimes?

'After she was struck, she was then strangled. There was no sign that she fought back, no sexual assault, but she was stripped naked.'

John Reeves thought for a minute. 'Did we get her clothes?'

'No, sir, just like the others, she was left naked and there was no sign of her clothes, shoes, handbag or personal belongings.' Finally her boss was starting to ask questions. Was this finally a break in his distracted mood?

'Okay, Sandra, keep looking,' he said, 'surely someone's got something. Get the journalists involved as well, and keep door-knocking, it's bound to turn up something.'

Sandra retreated to the media office. She, too, was perplexed about the clothes. Why would someone take all the women's clothes? Maybe it was because of possible DNA evidence. She guessed that was probably it.

After passing on the information to the journalists so it could hit the evening papers, she looked more closely at the CCTV footage.

The first woman had been wearing plain office attire, but her style shone through in her killer heels, which were emerald green suede. Beautiful, Sandra thought.

The second woman had a little more panache with her snugly fitted peacock-blue skirt suit. Her matching briefcase was elegant and expensive looking.

The third victim was clearly unfamiliar with the corporate world, judging by her dress standard. Denim-blue straight-leg pants, flat black pumps and a pale pink mohair jumper were hardly corporate wear.

John Reeves bellowed from his office for her to join him. She was so focused on the footage she nearly fell off her chair. Breathless from sprinting along the corridor, she bolted into her boss's office. 'Yes, sir, did you want me, sir?'

'Yes, detective sergeant, sit down a minute, I've got an assignment for you.'

As Sandra was pondering the thought of adding another assignment to her already overloaded agenda, her boss began to speak.

'So, here's the thing. We don't seem to be getting anywhere fast with these assaults-slash-murders. We need to take more definitive action, and we need you on board with this.' John Reeves stared coldly straight into Sandra's eyes.

She didn't dare flinch or look away. 'Yes, sir,' was all she could manage.

John Reeves continued. 'I need you to ride the six-ten train from the city and walk the path our victims walked. I need you to be bait. Do you understand? I need us to catch this guy. Think you're up to it?'

Sandra gulped. Before she could start doubting her own abilities, or her confidence in carrying out this bizarre but not totally unexpected task, she nodded in the affirmative.

'Good,' said her somewhat miserable boss. 'Good. Make it Friday evening. PC Morrison will masquerade as a train guard, and PC Allen will wait near the car park. You'll be quite safe. Okay with that?'

Again, Sandra nodded. Her mind was going ten to the dozen. What if no one saves me? What if they get there too late? What if it's all over before I can yell out? Sandra's private thoughts were taking over her usually rational thought processes and she had to stop herself mid thought by directing her next question audibly to her boss.

'What should I wear?'

John Reeves blinked at her as if he couldn't believe what he was hearing. 'Wear something you usually would, something that says corporate office.'

Sandra thought of the last victim, who really could have used a lesson in fashion coordination.

Friday evening came around fast. The stage was apparently set, according to Sandra's boss. John Reeves had been in constant communication all day, and she had raided her wardrobe for her best corporate look. Grey wool pants, silver silk shirt and red tailored jacket. Her Italian-leather shoes in the coolest grey topped off the look. She teamed it all with a grey leather clutch and she was ready.

She was a little nervous. On reflection, she wasn't sure that it was the smartest move of her career to be used as bait for a maniacal killer. Still, she wanted to get ahead, so she would have to suck it up and take one for the team. That's the story she was telling her subconscious over and over again in the hope that soon she would believe it.

Her job was important to her. She planned on climbing the ladder and one day taking her boss's place as head of investigations. She doubted that John Reeves would be there much longer anyway. The superintendent had been visiting a lot lately, and her boss never looked happy afterwards. The super always had a wink and a smile for her, though.

Boarding the six-ten train from the city, and taking a seat midway through the second carriage, Sandra caught herself looking around at the other passengers. She wondered if the bald-headed man three rows in front of her was the killer. He looked strong enough. She caught the eye of the distinguished-looking forty-something businessman opposite her, and for a fleeting moment felt his eyes undressing her. Oh my, she thought, is he the one?

She turned her attention to the opposite side of the train, where two young blokes were laughing at pictures on a phone. Sandra caught the odd word here and there, which didn't help to dispel the growing fear in her belly.

'Deserved it,' said one.

'Check out that body,' said the other.

'I could go that, couldn't you?' said the first, followed by guttural laughter.

Sandra was becoming nervous. There seemed to be so many possible suspects aboard this train. Perhaps one of them was the killer, or perhaps none of them was the killer and she was safe.

Sandra's phone rang; it was her boss.

'Sandra, you okay?' John Reeves said. 'Did you make the train? Don't worry, we'll get the guy if he's out there. You'll be safe, I guarantee it.'

'I know,' she mumbled quietly. 'Thanks.' Then she followed it with an audible, 'I'm on the train, see you at home, darling.'

Sandra reflected on the knowledge that she wasn't expected home, and that no one was waiting for her. Perhaps her mother had been right. There was no chance of a romantic relationship while she was so focused on her career.

After putting the phone in her bag—making sure she was still connected to her boss, a ploy they had agreed on earlier—Sandra looked at her hands. Her nails were impeccable. She'd had the acrylic applied by an expert yesterday. They were a lovely soft grey to match her shoes. She wanted to look the part of killer bait, and draw attention to herself for the right reasons.

The train pulled into the station and Sandra drew in a sharp breath. This was it!

As she stood and smoothed her trousers the way a well-dressed woman would, she noticed the bald man alighting from the carriage. The two young blokes, who were still laughing raucously, followed closely behind him.

It's now or never, thought Sandra. She moved towards the open sliding doors and stepped onto the platform. She looked straight ahead, and headed for the path that could very well lead her to her death. How could her boss guarantee her safety?

The two young blokes retrieved old pushbikes and were riding off in the opposite direction. Sandra let go of the breath she was unaware had been trapped in her lungs. It feels better to breath, she thought.

Sandra lost sight of the bald-headed man as she entered the dimly lit path leading to the car park. She could hear her heart beating loudly in her ears. She couldn't see or hear anyone else, and instantly she felt alone and abandoned. She tried to slow her breath, and strained her ears for any sounds that might emerge and put her at ease, but none came.

Halfway down the path, she heard a noise behind her, and then another just the same. She tried to still her thoughts to identify the sound, which she was sure she'd heard it many times before. Then she identified it: high heels clicking on a concrete path.

Sandra turned and tried to focus on the sound behind her. As her eyes adjusted to the dark, the first thing she saw was a pair of high-heel shoes. They were emerald-green suede, and stunning. As Sandra tried to remember where she had seen those shoes before, she let her eyes travel further to the torso of the wearer of the shoes. A lovely peacock-blue skirt was matched with the palest-of-pinks mohair jumper. The woman carried an expensive and attractive briefcase.

Sandra's heart stopped momentarily as reality dawned. Those clothes belonged to the victims. Surely this woman couldn't be the killer.

But what if the killer was a woman—*this* woman, who was wearing the beautiful clothes she had taken from her victims?

As the woman came closer, swinging the briefcase, Sandra used her tactical-response training and tackled her to the ground.

'Hey!' yelled the woman. 'What the hell are you doing? Let me go!'

Sandra kept a tight hold on the woman in the palest-of-pinks mohair jumper as PC Morrison leapt out of the bushes, offering assistance.

'Where did you get these clothes?' Sandra said to the handcuffed woman. The idea of this svelte, mouthy, uneducated woman being the killer was rapidly diminishing; the woman was shaking in her gorgeous shoes and crying all over her slim-line skirt.

The woman was beside herself. 'I-I found them,' she stammered through her tears. There was no way she was going to tell the cops about the man who had given her the parcel of drycleaned clothes. He'd told her that there was more coming, so she was going to stick to her story and tell the police she'd found them.

Realising that she wasn't getting any sense out of the woman, Sandra instructed PC Morrison to take her to the station for further questioning. At the very least, they had the victim's clothes for DNA testing. Hopefully something would come out of this that would help get them closer to the real killer.

As the uniformed constables walked to the waiting squad car with the woman, Sandra rummaged in her bag to retrieve her phone. She was surprised to see that her boss had disconnected the call. So much for him staying on the line, she thought. Lucky she hadn't needed him.

At the same time that Sandra was on her way back to the station, John Reeves was in the hospital on the other side of town, keeping vigil at the bedside of a woman in a coma. He gently stroked her hair and leaned in to whisper in her ear.

'You know,' he said softly, 'I can't stand the way that woman dresses. Dress to impress, they say. Well, let me tell you that no woman should dress that way to get ahead in her job. You shouldn't have, either, and that's why you're here. You were too sassy for your own good. Bet your boss was worried about you taking his job, too. Well, no chance of that now. Not in the state you're in, my girl. I can't let you live now, can I? As soon as you open those beautiful eyes you'll be telling tales on me, won't you? But I don't think you'll be waking up anytime soon.'

John Reeves leaned in closer to the comatose woman, and placed his hand over her nose and mouth. The monitor on the wall began making a buzzing sound, then the woman's vital statistics flatlined. Before the nurses swarmed in to investigate, John Reeves slipped quietly away.

He needed to rest. Tomorrow he would continue his quest to provide his successor with a case she wouldn't solve in a hurry. He might be old, but he had many years on her when it came to perfect murders.

The Phone Call

Anita Howard

They were used to cars parked across the road from their home. They were used to a person watching, observing and analysing what was happening at their family address.

They were used to phone calls with heavy breathing or silence.

The police had instructed them to pick up the ringing phone, say 'Yes' and then listen until the caller hung up.

The police said the caller would verbalise their anger instead of coming to their home.

The police told her, as the eldest child (at sixteen), that when her parents were not home she should always answer the phone as if she was their mother.

They were often left alone, she, her sister and her two brothers.

They were prepared with pepper, a saucepan and rope—their tools of defence placed ready for action by the front door.

They ate their dinner, watched television and went to bed.

She closed her eyes, and as she lay in her bed she listened to the creaks and groans of their home as it, too, settled for the night.

She opened her eyes and sighed with frustration at the sound of the phone. She hugged her pillow around her head to block the sound.

She slipped her feet into slippers, her arms into the sleeves of her dressing gown, and dragged her feet towards her parents' bedroom and the unrelenting ring of the phone.

'Yes,' she said, into the receiver.

'Is that fucking Mrs Nobbs?' a male voice shouted.

'Yes,' she said.

'Is your fucking husband there?'

'No.'

'Fuck! Youse'll just 'ave to fucking tell 'im, right?'

'Yes.'

'Now, youse fucking listen. I knows your fucking brats, two boys and two girls. Now's because of your fucking husband. I'm gonna tie youse up and youse fucking husband.'

Silence.

'Are youse still fucking there?'

'Yes.' She swallowed her panic and suspended her fear in a jelly of numbness.

He continued, and she listened.

He kept stopping to check that she was still listening, occasionally asking her to repeat what he had just said.

She'd say a little, stopping when a word was too disturbing for her to say, hoping she'd said enough to show she was listening.

He told her, with detailed descriptions, how he would start with her youngest son, strip him, rape him, then cut him and leave him to bleed. This act he would repeat for the next son and the two daughters.

Throughout, the word 'fucking' punctuated his spiteful words.

In her mind, she sang nursery rhymes — *Mary had a little lamb, little lamb, little lamb* — in an attempt to block out his words.

Then she heard him sigh. 'That was great,' he said in a more normal tone. 'I could keep talking, but I wanna do it for fucking real. So, Mrs Nobbs, youse knows I fucking knows where youse live and I'm gonna come *now!*'

She heard the click on the line as the man hung up.

She heard the sounds of night: owls, cars and dogs.

She looked at the receiver as it slid through her fingers and dropped — *crash* — onto the wooden floor. Shivering, she climbed under her parents' doona.

All she could hear and think was: *I'm gonna come now!*

She didn't want to be the eldest.

She didn't want to answer the phone calls.

She didn't want to be responsible for her sister and brothers.

A flood of questions pierced her consciousness.

What should I do?

Who should I tell?

Who should I ring?

She wanted someone there, *now.* She wanted someone to take control. She wanted someone to ...

She opened the address book, scanning their neighbours' names. With a shaky finger, she pressed the numbers.

'Hello, Mr Johns, help! Please come here ... to our house ... *now.*' She spoke through gasps of air and all-consuming sobs.

She heard a 'Yes' and heaved a sigh of relief.

She raced downstairs and turned on the light outside the front door. Gathered a saucepan, pepper and rope, then crouched trembling in the corner by the door, waiting for Mr Johns' voice.

Through her mind raced angry questions.

Why do Mum and Dad have to go out all the time?

Why does Dad have to defend these people?

Why can't the police stop them watching and calling us?

Why do I have to listen?

How do these horrible men know where we live?

How do they know our phone number?

How am I ever going to get his voice out of my head?

A car engine stopped ... a door creaked ... a door slammed ... footsteps, two lots of footsteps ...

She had expected Mr Johns to walk from his house, but maybe he had come by car. Or maybe it was the man on the phone ... and someone else. Who did the second set of footsteps belong to?

She made herself as small as she could, closed her eyes and willed it not to be the man on the phone. She waited ... the footsteps were louder, closer ... they stopped on the other side of the door. She held her breath ...

Knock-knock.

'Sue, are you there? It's Mr Johns.'

She raised her body, reached out and turned the door handle.

'You caused us some embarrassment last night,' Mum said.

'But the phone call was—' she started to say.

'Yes, I heard. Mr Johns described the state you were in when he arrived and how he gave you some brandy to stop you from shaking.'

'I was terrified, the phone call—'

'Yes, Mr Johns told us. That's why he drove, he said, in case he needed to take someone to the hospital. He told us you described the call to him, and because you still seemed frightened he stayed till we came home. Can you imagine how surprised we were to find him here?'

'But I was—'

'Yes, look, you've only had one of these calls, but I've had many of them. Just forget about it,' Mum said.

She had wanted her mum to give her a hug, to reassure and comfort her; to listen to how she felt and then give her another hug.

Instead she started taking aspirin to get to sleep, one, two, three … whatever worked.

That helped her at night, but during the day the man's voice played in her head. She felt anxious, and tried filling her days with activities so there was no time to think, no time to focus on the voice. But it was still there.

By accident, she found that scratching mosquito bites helped. She scratched over and over, until they hurt, until they bled.

This pain was stronger than the voice.

Warning Labels

Kylie Thompson

The video comes via my daughter, so of course I snatch up my phone and click on the link. Like always, it starts with blackness, like she's left her phone in her pocket and accidentally hit record, or like she's smuggling her camera into position. Helena has been sending me videos all week, little sweet snippets of her day, because she's worried I'm too focused on my books and imagined bodies to remember that the real world isn't as terrible as the world inside my head.

She swears I'm getting too morbid. She might have a point. It doesn't matter how much I play up the affable writer mum for the media, the truth is that kind, gentle souls make terrible crime writers, and I'm not even close to mediocre. You stay in this biz long enough, you learn to enjoy the carnage you bring to the page; start to get a sick— probably at least a little psychologically concerning—thrill at the gore you imagine into being.

No wonder we all end up on watch lists.

I'm the sort of person who thinks that writing murder scenes is therapeutic. Helena's the sort of kid who believes in adding sunshine to someone else's day. If I hadn't seen her give blood, I'd swear her red stuff was actually glitter and rainbows. There are moments of attitude, of course, because she's a teenager, not a saint. But then she'll wander in and tell me to clean my workspace, like I'm the wayward child in the house, and I'll be struck, again, by how unalike we are.

I gave birth to a daughter, and yet sometimes, more often than I'd care to admit, I wonder if the girl I raised is really mine. It wouldn't matter if there'd been a mix-up in the maternity ward; Helena is mine in every way that matters. But the thing is, she's sweet; the kind of sweet I've never managed, and her daddy certainly never did. Practical, patient, and kind; all the things her parents never were. So how the hell does a sweet kid like that come from two such ornery fuck-ups?

Being at opposite ends of the personality spectrum doesn't matter. I love her. I even love the damn videos. I assume it'll be another lunch at the pond in the park, periwinkle-blue lilies in bloom and the old black swan waddling, drunken and still somehow a little threatening, towards her for food.

Or maybe it's the street-corner poet again, the one who creates poems about the people passing him by. She's carried a torch for him for years, and, judging by his poems to her, she's not alone in that. Even I'm starting to ship it.

What I don't expect is a close-up of an eye. Muddy green, so familiar that I feel my heart stutter at the sight of it. Helena's eye. Her carefully applied mascara and liner is smeared and running with her tears; her face is swollen and bruising.

There's a mule-kick of rage, hardening in the back of my throat and clenching my hands into claws, like I'm gonna rip someone's eye clear out of its socket and slap them with it if there's not an explanation in thirty seconds or less.

The image lingers, the only movement the slow blackened slide of tears and her blinks, while my brain does the math from 'What the fuck, is she pranking me?' to 'She'd never be this cruel' to a slide home into 'Some bastard's got my kid'.

The video came as a surprise; the surge of rage, not so much. The rage is good. It keeps the urge to throw up at bay, stops the tears and screaming before they have a chance to steal my focus. Cry later. Save your baby girl now. I don't know how, though.

Treat it like a story. Cop school 101.

What do you do?

I don't know!

Think. Assume he's smart until proven otherwise. How does he stop you sending this to the police?

He makes sure only I can see it.

The world still feels like it speeds and slows and twists around me, her eye filling my screen, and then I'm scrambling for the spare phone in my drawer, random junk flying everywhere, thumbing on the phone and waiting aeons for it to start up.

Oh god, let it be charged.

Pantheons of gods I don't even believe in are clearly on my side today; it loads in record time, doesn't freeze as I hit record and position the camera over my phone's screen.

It's not perfect—the image is scarred with checkerboard pixilation—but it'll do.

For another minute, her eye stares unseeing and desperate, and then the camera pulls shakily outwards in an accidental *Blair Witch* homage that owes more to shitty camerawork than artistry.

Her face is pale, the left side in worse shape than the right now that I can see it all. More bruises. Either she hadn't come quietly—likely—or the sadist responsible is due a boot fair in the balls—definitely. A trickle of blood, long since clotted and dried, trails from a minor wound at her scalp. Her eyes are, thankfully, aware, if wide and terrified.

When Hel was seven, she cracked her head open playing cricket with her father. As we sat in the ER, breathing in that toxic-cleanliness smell, the doctor stitching her skin back together, Hel stared at me like that. The only word she could manage through the tears was 'Mum', like a prayer, like I could stop the pain and fear with just a word, or a touch. Like I could magic it all away.

Her favourite glittery aqua scarf has been shoved into her mouth and tied around her head to keep her quiet, and I wonder if she'd be calling out my name now if she could. I force my hand to unclench, to hold the spare phone in a safer grip. Jam my elbows into my sides to minimise my own shaky camerawork.

The cameraman has figured out that he doesn't have all day to get this done. There's an awkward fumble, and the phone in his hand points to a laptop screen. Another phone fumble while he turns on his presentation, and this might actually be the stupidest kidnapping ever. I'm a little surprised there's no music in his PowerPoint presentation. It's the usual don't-call-the-cops shtick, his voice aiming for menacing and low, but mostly just sounding like it hurts to maintain that pitch, like a kid pretending to be Batman.

If I focus on the absurdity, maybe I won't throw up. Gallows humour and all that.

Though the slideshow of pictures of mutilated bodies is half-hearted and overpopulated with screenshots of Google searches, it makes his point rather effectively.

The back of my throat is acrid with bile and rage, but if I scream or cry I'm never going to stop. I jam my thumbnail into the palm of my hand until the surge of emotion lessens to manageable. The crescent of blood is easy enough to ignore.

Another jerky camera reposition, followed by a tantalising glimpse of shitty, graffitied brickwork and shittier lighting. A warehouse. Really? You take a crime writer's kid and opt for villainy cliche? Where's the goddamned artistry?

This? Not the actions of a supervillain. It shouldn't make me angrier, but it does.

His face fills the screen, gets smaller as he fumbles for the right angle; posturing like he's twenty-eight kinds of badass. He looks like a high schooler trying out for a role in the school play, or unnamed thug #8 in a really shitty movie.

The Batman voice doesn't help. 'Your daughter has twenty-four hours. You will bring five million dollars to a location we specify. You will come alone. We are monitoring your phones. If you call the police, we will know and Helena will die. We will not negotiate. Do not try our patience.'

We, 'like it's not a one-man operation, like he's not holding the damn phone himself. And he sure as hell doesn't have helpers in the building. No one selfies the ransom video if they don't have to.

The screen flickers back to Helena for a moment, then fades to black.

It's almost funny the way he thinks I'd go to the cops. That I'd choose to obey a chain of command when I already have access to all of their resources, without any of that serve-and-protect bullshit to stand in my way. Like I'd sit around and hope someone else gets to my daughter in time.

Idiot should read a goddamned book.

There should be a PSA on the jackets of my books: *Warning: I plan inventive ways to kill people for a living. Targeting my kid will end badly for you.*

Granted, the media love playing on the sweet-woman-with-a-killer-streak shtick, and I work hard to keep the rep of easy-going fan favourite. Affable folk? Not known for their violent tendencies. But affable people who kill people in fiction for a living tend to be hiding a multitude of rages beneath their politely interested smiles.

And the ones rich enough to walk into any weapons shop anywhere in the world and buy whatever they want, no questions asked? We should seriously have warning labels.

After Helena's father, there was the obligatory string of mistakes. Some try to stay in touch now I've got money, but there's only one I'm actually friends with. Jackson is the kind of guy who aspires to be a black hat, but will never come close to managing it. Oh, sure, he hacks for fun, karma and profit, but those profits get funnelled straight into women's shelter donations and saving starving kids in Third World countries. The guy makes Robin Hood look half-assed.

He's also the sort of paranoid that demanded I accept a phone he'd purchased, a burner for an emergency. I've never been more grateful for the Boy Scout preparedness that used to drive me crazy. The second the video ends, I dial his number on the spare phone. He'll help. He loves Hel like she's his own damn kid.

He answers on the third ring, voice distant while he works on one of his projects.

'Some asshole took Helena.'

That gets his attention. He's on it in a goddamned heartbeat, tracing the call and already trying to turn on the geolocation function on her phone. His voice is shaky, scared and furious, and so much like a father's that I wish, not for the first time, that Hel was really his kid.

'Is she hurt?'

'Bruised. Cut to the head.' He can't see me gesturing stupidly, unsure of the full extent of her injuries. Can't see the lack of tears, or the way my foot keeps twitching like it's itching to kick out at someone. He can't see the shaking, but I don't doubt he hears it in my voice. Out of everyone I've ever known—even Hel's dad—Jackson's the one who knows me. He doesn't need to see any of it to hear the unspoken. 'There's video,' I add.

'Good. Get over here, we'll figure this out. We'll find her, Cass.'

I always thought that saying someone 'growled' was just shitty, melodramatic writing. But the sound Jackson makes as he sees Hel's teary face is that of a possessed dog in a horror movie. If he could leap through the screen, I'm pretty sure he'd earn that black hat.

He watches the video five times, pinpointing the perfect stills to search from, and then he's off and racing, fingers dancing over keyboards, worrying his bottom lip between his teeth as he looks towards my daughter's miserable face. I spend the first four of Jackson's replays pointedly ignoring the screen, surveying his creepily clean kingdom. It's unnatural, the amount of dust-free shined-to-hell surfaces in one shitty little apartment.

I keep my hands pressed against my ears, humming softly to drown out the video until Jackson shakes my shoulder to get my attention.

'What's the play?'

'Get her back,' I say.

He shoots me a look, the sort of look I'm sure he taught Helena when she was young enough to learn to be sensible. 'What would you suggest?' he asks. 'Cops?' A snort of laughter from the hacker, unsurprising given he's hacking the cops' databases.

In the screen's reflection his expression shifts from amused to worried. 'You're getting in some muscle, right? This isn't some maternal kamikaze deal, is it?' The sound of his fingers smacking keys doesn't falter, just gets louder like it's the closest he can get to punching something right now. 'It won't do her a damned bit of good if you get yourself offed pretending you're Wonder Woman.'

It's easy enough to lie to him when his gaze shifts back to the still of Hel's face, like he can't stop himself. 'Of course I'm bringing gunhands. I'm not an idiot.' He's too worried to remember that 'idiot' should be my middle name when it comes to Helena.

Coming here is risky enough. Adding more players if I'm really being watched is the quickest way to get Helena killed. Study true crime long enough, you get good and jaded about the worthwhile nature of emergency collaboration.

It doesn't take long for Jackson to find the guy, because the genius kidnapper doesn't bother wearing a mask, or trying to hide his identity. Seriously, even scribbling black Texta over his face would be better than the lack of effort.

Ivan Peterson. Twenty-nine. Not your intellectual kind of bad guy; definitely more thug #8 than supervillain. He's not known for his kidnappings, not a shocker given the dodgy efforts he's made. Jail time for violent home invasions, but not as much as there should be.

Implicated in a number of murders, but Ivan has himself a guardian angel dragging his ass out of the fire when needed.

Interesting. Could I have pissed someone off?

It's likely.

There are sealed files from a wayward youth—again, not a shocker—and Jackson doesn't even stop to shoot me a triumphant smile the way he used to. He just keeps working.

'Little Ivan was the sort of kid the neighbourhood pets hated,' he says. 'Probably had something to do with his habit of tryin' to dissect 'em in the middle of the night. It got him thrown into the in-patient time-out corner. Not for long, but enough to learn to smile and be a charming little asshole who can pretend that making people suffer doesn't give him a tickle.'

Jackson frowns, scanning the screen, and when he starts speaking again, his voice is scratched and broken to hell. 'Ivan likes to make people scream. And not in a fun kinda way.'

Judging by his white-knuckled grip on the desk's edge, I'm not the only one contemplating what that means for Hel. I barely make it to the rubbish bin before I'm losing breakfast, and probably five years of childhood memories, in the purge. Jackson just hands me his bottle of water when I'm done.

'What about the warehouse?' I say. 'Can you trace it?'

'From what? The tagging? Pu-lease. I can do better than that.' He shoots me a wrecked parody of that triumphant grin as a property deed flashes onto the screen. 'Daddy dearest left the failed family business to him. One old, shitty warehouse for your consideration.' He scrawls the address onto a Post-it note, hands it over. 'Promise me you're not going alone, Cass.' That earnest, worried expression breaks my damn heart.

'I just want Hel back. I'm not out to kick ass and take names. That's for my characters, not reality.'

He smiles, relieved. Doesn't try to keep me talking, just lets me dash away with nothing more than a 'Call me when she's safe' that stops me in my tracks.

'Screw that,' I say. 'You know where the spare key is. Come over for dinner, see she's safe for yourself.'

'I'll bring the food. You bring the happily-ever-after moment, yeah?'

Damn right.

My first book, *Pistol Ali*, was about a kidnapping ring. Months of research, hours transcribing interviews with retired cops and PIs, trying to get a feel for the problems my heroine, Ali, would face. And in the end, it came down to one throwaway comment by a half-drunk ex-cop. Kidnappers? If they're not hiding their faces, they're not planning to let their hostages walk away, or the idiot holding the ransom.

And with that morbid little thought, oddly I know it's all going to be okay. Sick bastards with agendas; I've been writing them since I was old enough to give my English teacher nightmares. I can deal with doublecrosses. I do it every day for work. It's daily life that screws me up.

I've kept a black-market gun hidden in a hollowed out copy of *Pistol Ali* ever since I could afford to buy the damned thing. It's easy to load, tested enough that I know it's trustworthy.

The holster from my gun safe conceals almost perfectly around my ankle. I strap the sheathed dagger I bought in Asia from a man claiming to be a Samurai tightly around my wrist, changing into a long-sleeved hoodie to better hide the sheath. I grab a coat, dark colours just in case. As long as nobody hugs me no one will notice a thing.

It takes me almost no time to organise a backpack of clothes, some for me, some for Helena, and to throw in some bleach and gloves. There's petrol in the car, a lighter in my purse.

It's all gonna be okay.

It's the usual rundown building, and I'm pretty sure I'm gonna stab Ivan for the sheer cliche of it all. It's in the bad part of town that the bad part of town tries to avoid; although the buildings are tagged to hell there's no sign of life, like even the squatters thought better of lingering. My car stands out, or it would if anyone was looking. Out of all the derelict shitholes on the street, Ivan's is the most rundown, the front door almost falling from its hinges.

Not an option. I don't need to drop steel on my head, or let him know I'm coming.

It's not a huge warehouse; it takes no time to do a lap, ducking beneath windows and staying to the shadows.

KYLIE THOMPSON: WARNING LABELS

There are multiple entrances, but no security cameras anywhere. There's no hired help keeping an eye out for trouble, no one to beat into submission. No bodies to hide.

It's disappointing, truth be told, to just pick a lock on the side door and wander inside.

There's ranting, though, a barely-there thrum of sound out of place with the dilapidated calm of the building. Better than GPS for finding morons.

I'd never assumed the bastard was smart. And there he is, in front of Hel, monologuing like he's a goddamn character from Shakespeare. Her head is lowered, her one good eye scrunched in fury. I know that look. That's the look she gets when she's fighting the urge to call someone words she's a little embarrassed to admit she knows.

There's too much chance of missing the shot, and shooting my daughter because my hands are shaking isn't how this day is going to end. Dagger, definitely the dagger; it glides, silent as a wraith, from its sheath.

He doesn't even notice me walking up behind him. Neither does Helena.

I don't try to get Hel's attention, to let her know it's going to be okay. Right now, Cassie St Samael isn't here. Right now there's no room for affable writers, only vengeful mothers.

It would be easier, of course, to slit his throat before he knows I'm here. And if Ivan was the head idiot behind this, I probably would. But he's the hired help, and there are larger whales requiring harpoons up the ass today.

There's a list of options in my head: a hundred ways to bring him to his knees, to take control of the situation. Any and all could be fun. Perks of the job: I know how to make him fall into line. Hell, a hard enough hit to the head would do it, but if I'm honest, I want to make him hurt. I want to make him scream the way he's made so many others scream.

So instead I reach up, grab an ear and cut it from his head. The scream catches Helena's attention. I ignore her muffled shouting. If I look at her, I'll stop. I'll call the police. I'll be good.

As he spins to face his attacker I punch the bastard right in the nose. It cracks, loud even over his shouting, and while the son of a bitch is trying to figure out whether to hold his nose or his ear, I nail him, hard, in the balls.

Ivan, clutching a rather severe case of retractus marblus, screams like a little girl.

He was gonna make my little girl scream.

One little kick pushes him onto the ground, where he hunches in pain. It takes a broken finger to get his attention back to where it's needed.

'You took my daughter away from me.'

Ivan shakes his head fast, too fast, as though if he can deny it strongly enough, maybe I'll believe. I throw on my best affable grin. The warm patches on my face make me think it's a little more blood spattered than I'd usually wear it.

'Bad idea, that,' I say. 'But I'm nothing if not forgiving. Was anybody else involved in this?'

'No.'

I grab his broken finger, wrench it just a bit until he sobs. 'Are you completely, entirely sure about that, Ivan? Because you strike me as the hired help, not the brains. So I'm going to oh-so-generously ask you one last time. Then I'm going to make you tell me the truth. Spoiler: it won't be pleasant.'

'You can't touch me.' He's trying, failing, for bravado, and this, right here, is why I doubt he's the criminal mastermind of the day.

I break another finger, just to prove the point, keeping eye contact and grin in place as I do. It shouldn't be easy to smile at him, but it is.

'The blood all over you seems to disprove that theory, but still, let's discuss. You took my fucking daughter, you piece of shit. You hurt her, you tied her up, and you kept her here against her will. And if you've been paying attention, you'll have realised that I didn't go to the police, Ivan. You know why?'

He shakes his head, fast, like a scared child, eyes wide and teary.

'Because they have rules. They don't believe in cutting your fucking fingers off one at a damned time until you tell me the truth. They won't kill you. Me? I'll kill you. Slowly. And I'll smile the whole damn time. So answer me this, Ivan-the-grunt, how did I make my money?'

He answers slowly, unsure of himself for the first time in the conversation. 'Writing?'

I throw him my best patient-schoolteacher smile. 'And what do I write?'

'Crime ...'

'Don't say it like that, like it's a hobby. Like I'm collecting fucking doilies or something. Show some goddamn respect. I have spent my adult life thinking up ways to torture and kill, and you think I'll get squeamish about making a grunt like you talk? Think on that, if you will.'

There's nothing left of his bravado but a violently shaking aftertaste, and I leave him to contemplate his life choices while I move to Helena, not daring to look too closely at her injuries. I need answers before my primal therapy session kicks off.

'I'm gonna cut you free, okay?' She nods, eyes wide, minute gestures still somehow frantic, and it takes no time to move behind her, to untie the scarf and cut away the bindings. 'I need you to stay where you are for a few minutes, okay, sweetie?'

She shoots me a scowl at the overly calm mum voice, like even smacked about and kidnapped she can't quite ditch the teen attitude. Again a nod, though she sets about rubbing at her wrists, trying to get feeling back in her hands. She moves her jaw like she's trying to get feeling back there, too. Clearly, I don't have long before there's a voice of reason in play. Time's running out, even if it's a pretty safe bet Helena won't be able to walk for a little while.

I kick out at Ivan as I move back to him, catch him in the kidneys and let him groan for a moment before grabbing a fistful of hair and dragging him over to face me. I have maybe a few minutes left of this rush of adrenaline. Then all I'll have is rage to fuel me.

I think I'll be okay.

'Have you had enough time to think about things, Ivan? Because if you've ever read any of my work—and I hope you have—it's quite good. You'll know just how creative I can be. You tell me who you're working for and I won't torture it out of you.'

For a moment, it looks like he'll refuse. He looks determined, stupidly so. And then he looks into my eyes and shudders. Actually shudders. His shoulders droop.

'His name is Stephens. Jonas Stephens.'

Unexpected. The name is painfully familiar. A friend. Former. A former friend about to have a very bad, blood-spattered-day kind of friend.

'Are you sure you're telling me everything?' Ivan nods, the desperately earnest kind of nod usually reserved for toddlers and drunks. 'Okay, then.' I raise the knife, ignoring the shout.

'But you promised!'

Can't quite ignore Helena's shout, though.

'Mum, wait!' She's stumbling a bit as she walks, but she still moves fast for someone who's spent the better part of the day tied to a chair.

'You tell me to call the cops,' I say, 'and you're grounded till you're eighty.'

She laughs, though it's well on its way to hysteria. Between and below us, Ivan-the-grunt is looking at Helena like she's goddamn Santa. I want to rip out his eyeballs, start making a list of all the ways I know to cut them from his head while he's awake enough to feel it.

'Give me the knife, Mum.' She holds out her hand expectantly, wearing the face she gets when she's the parent, not me. When she's talking me down from something ridiculous and stupid. The expression I'm one-hundred-percent sure Jackson taught her.

'He hit you. He ...' I gesture stupidly at her; blood soaked but somehow still looking patient and kind. 'And you want me to let him go? Let him do this to someone else?'

'Give me the knife, Mum.'

It's physically painful, but I've never been able to deny Helena. I've always trusted that expression, and I'm sure as hell not going to start saying no after she's been held hostage because of me. I flip the dagger carelessly, hand it to her hilt first.

Of course, I know Helena reads my books—after all, she's one of my favourite beta readers—but I never realised she'd been taking notes.

She slams the blade into Ivan's crotch with all the strength she can muster. I'm impressed at what she can do with hands shaking so badly. Wonder if she's been practising her accuracy. Ivan screams, writhes. Doesn't see the blade again until it's embedded in his stomach. He howls.

When I was ten, my dog got hit by a car. He howled like that. Like he knew he was dying and couldn't believe it. Helena keeps stabbing and I can't tell her to stop, mainly because she's doing exactly what I was going to do. Every wound is guaranteed to hurt like hell. There's no hesitation, no sympathy. Just fury.

Every so often, I wonder if Helena is truly mine, or if there was some mix-up at the hospital. It wouldn't matter if the DNA didn't match up of course, but there are moments when she is so unlike both of her parents that I can't help but wonder.

Right now, covered in blood and using her kidnapper as physical therapy, she's totally, irrevocably, my daughter.

Maybe the daughters of crime writers should have warning labels, too.

Contributors

Award winning author, **KAZ DELANEY**, and her alter ego, **KERRI LANE** have currently sold 75 books between them. Her books have been honoured with several awards including an ARRA award, an Aurealis Award, Best Children's Series, and Best  Education series as well as being long listed in the Davitt Awards.

Her award winning Young Adult novels are published by Allen & Unwin, the latest of which is a rural romance entitled *The Reluctant Jillaroo.* Her soon to be released *Holly Hart Mystery Series* is a cosy mystery series set in Texas, and takes her back to where she began – writing mysteries spiced with a little bit of romance for the adult market.

With her husband Bob she resides at beautiful Lake Macquarie on the NSW coast where she can indulge her love of both the beach and lake.

You can find Kaz at
www.kazdelaney.com.au *and*
www.facebook.com/Kaz-Delaney-author

GEORGINA BALLANTINE, spends her days as a professional editor and author, working her magic on words and whimsy. When not chasing after her three spirited preteens, a paranoid dog and two vampire cats, she hides in her cupboard under the stairs, writing myth-based historical fantasy for adults and children. The opening of her alternate history/fantasy novel-in-progress *Foxfire* won the 2017 CYA Conference Prize (YA category).

Georgina has over twenty years' experience in the publishing industry as a freelance editor and writer. She co-manages the Australian Science Fiction and Fantasy Writers' Association, convenes a speculative fiction writers group and is a committee member of the Australian Fair Tale Society.

Georgina holds a BA Honours in Classics (Ancient Greek and Latin) and BSc in Environmental Science and Botany.

Website: www.georginaballantine.com
Facebook: facebook.com/georgina.ballantine
Twitter: twitter.com/GBBallantine
Instagram: www.instagram.com/georginaballantine/
LinkedIn: www.linkedin.com/in/georginaballantine/

My name is **LUKE WEST** and if you can do me one favour today, don't judge me on the opening sentence of this bio.

I love words, in a weird way and have always been fascinated by them. The fact it only takes a mixture of 26 letters to form a story that could potentially stick with you for life is mind blowing, right?

I like to use my passion for words to create contemporary fiction, usually aimed at young adult audience. Occasionally (usually during my man period) I put my characters through challenges outside of the contemporary confinements (put them through hell and back).

Thank you for using your time to take a chance on my stories. I hope you enjoy my world.

You can contact me on
luke.west87@icloud.com

TANIA COSSICH, lives in Melbourne, Australia, and draws from the wide wild world of wackiness to create characters in fancy flights of fiction and enjoys freeing them from her mind into unsuspecting print.

She has published non-fiction and journal articles and now draws from the wide wild world of words to create stories. Tania is a neophytic writer with a soft spot for alliteration, this is her first published story. Her imagination is both fuelled and tolerated by family, friends and fellow writers, to whom she offers her deep gratitude. May we all be safe from dark characters in bright pubs.

You can contact Tania on
Taniacossich@hotmail.com
for further information on her other works.

Ipswich author **CHARMAINE CLANCY**, loves to create characters for mystery, fantasy and adventure. She is Co-host and sometimes presenter for the Rainforest Writing Retreat.

When not explaining the dangers of underestimating a fairy or the best spots to hide a body, Charmaine also hosts creative writing clubs for children and produces online workshops for the classroom. As a teacher of literacy, Charmaine encourages children to engage with reading and writing through laughter and exploration. Her own books include My Zombie Dog, Dognapped? A Dog Show Detective Mystery and Undead Kev. She has won awards for her short stories and is published in anthologies.

Charmaine loves all things Agatha Christie and is often watching those around her with suspicious eyes; on the off chance they ever do commit a cleverly devised crime.

You can find Charmaine at
www.charmaineclancy.com

LIANE McDERMOTT, grew up in a small, one pub country town amidst the cane fields in North Queensland. She now lives in Brisbane with her husband, two children, two bantam chickens and a humanoid mini fox terrier named Max.
When not writing journal articles, reports or grant applications for her research work, Liane tries to fulfil her creative writing passion, which has mostly been in the realm of junior fiction and picture books. While this is her first publication in adult fiction, Liane has written a number of short stories and completed a Graduate Certificate in Creative Writing at the Queensland University of Technology.

You can contact Liane on
lj_mcdermott@yahoo.com.au

MARTII MACLEAN, lives in a tin shack by the sea, catching sea-gulls which she uses to make delicious pies, and writing weird stories. She likes going for long bicycle rides with her cat, who always wears aviator goggles to stop her whiskers  blowing up into her eyes as they speed down to the beach to search for mermaid eggs.

Martii writes fantastical, adventurous tales for children and teens, and sometimes adults. She actually lives in Brisbane with her husband Trevor and her cat Minerva. Her work as an educator and librarian, allows her to share her love of books and story-telling with young people and this has inspired her to write stories that explore the wonderful world of *'what if'*, including: If I Die Before I Wake, We of the Between, Weird Weirder Weirdest, The Adventures of Isabelle Necessary and Unreal Time.

Find out more at
www.martiimaclean.com

PAUL SMITH, is recently retired and started writing his first novel *"Walk with the Tiger"* not long after. This is the first adventure/thriller book in the **Jack Harrigan series** that is set in the seventies.

Paul has also written two short stories, *"Monty & Tomatso"* (a hardboiled detective set against a gangster in the 50's) and *"Murder on the Mountain"*, Jack solves a murder at a recent writers Retreat. Paul dabbles in Bush Poetry, his latest is called *"Jack the Dancer"*, set in a country pub back in the 1930's. He came to town to be a shearer but he got in a fight, one that they still talk about today.

Paul is part of the Rainforest Writing Retreats crew assisting where he is needed from driving busses to making sure everybody has settled in to their accommodation. Apart from writing his other interests include his classic 1956 Desoto, military weapons and a fitness program to combat arthritis.

Find out more at
www.paulsmithauthor.com

KATHY CHILDS, began writing in her spare time as a hobby - one that quickly developed into a passion. She delights in writing short stories – some light and fanciful, others dark and disturbing, and when the mood takes her, delving into  Australia's history to draw out some of the interesting characters that lie in our past. Kathy has won, or been placed in, a number of short story competitions, and has been published both on line and in print.

Kathy took time away from her own writing in 2017/2018 to act as a judge for several short story awards and publications. She is now back at the keyboard and is eager to complete the final edit of her novel - *You Will Always Be My Number One* - a psychological thriller set in Melbourne.

Kathy's publications are available on her website
www.kathychilds.com.au

CHRIS RADGE, is an Australian novelist based in Brisbane, Queensland where she writes fulltime and is a part-time stay-at-home NanMa.

She is currently engaged in writing an Octology of YA Urban Fantasy books called the *Elder Scale Series*. She is also a Children's picture books writer with titles of *Where the Lost Things Go* and *Sneezes* to be published in 2018. A series of ten Tenpin bowling picture books is also in the works.

Chris is a NECA multiple award winning non-fiction writer for both Queensland and Australia. She has been an editor for a Medical Association Magazine and is also an editor, publisher and marketer for a well renowned designer of cloth dolls patterns distributed worldwide.

She is a member of QWC, Booklinks and looks forward to the Rainforest Writing Retreat every year and caters for morning and afternoon tea, and she's writing a recipe book.

When you add chicken salt to hot chips you don't just create a meal - you create a delicacy.

You can contact her at
chris.radge@bigpond.com.

Find out more at
www.chrisradge.com

CHRIS CHILDS, flirts with several genres in her creative writing (historical fiction, biography, autobiography and crime), influenced by:

1) A passion for recreating 19th century Australian stories that have long disappeared from our memories. (Chris is an accredited professional historian)
2) Undergraduate and masters degrees in psychology, biography and life writing
3) A love of reading classic and contemporary crime and mystery novels

Chris has had a number of short stories published in several on-line journals and anthologies. She won first prize in the 2015 Henry Lawson literature awards and was the 2017 Words of Wyndham local short story winner. Chris is also an enthusiastic reviewer of Australian historical fiction for the international journal, *Historical Novels Review*.

The Brisbane Strangler straddles all three genres: history (if you count the 1980s as historical), semi-autobiographical (not the murder bit!) and crime (the murder bit!).

You can find Chris at
chrischilds.writer@gmail.com

LEA SCOTT, has published three psychological thrillers, The Ned Kelly Game (2009), Eclipsed (2010) and One for All (2013). She acts as Chair of the Queensland Writers Centre and mentors new writers under their 'Writer's Surgery'  program. She has facilitated writing workshops and seminars and appeared at writing festivals throughout Australia and overseas.

She has acted as associate editor for a Special Issue of *TEXT Journal of Writing*. Lea is currently undertaking a PhD in Creative Writing and has also published academic research on writing about trauma and the transformative potential of creative writing.

Find out more at
www.leascott.com

DIANE K EDWARDS, is a writer of fictional works and proudly describes her style as multi-general. (Not sure if that is a word, but in Diane's world it is!) From fantasy YA to literary fiction, mysteries and a memoir, her works are varied and  interesting. Blessed with a vivid imagination Diane takes great delight in writing short stories and flash fiction plus has a novel manuscript awaiting final editing prior to publication.

Diane also writes travel blogs and specialty stories for special occasions. In a previous life Diane has written lyrics for over 30 songs and once her singing is up to scratch will eventually record an album! After spending the last 4 years living and working overseas Diane has returned to Brisbane and her normal day job as a Vocational Training Manager. In her spare time Diane is CEO of Vixen Publishing House – creating opportunities for Australian Authors to partner with registered charities for mutually beneficial gain.

You can contact Diane at
dke@dianekathrynedwards.com
www.vixenpublishing.com

ANITA HOWARD, is an artist, and writer. She has explored and worked in exotic and confronting places over decades, including Cambodia and Timor Leste (as a volunteer teacher). She has utilised experiences from these places and those from her life to  mould stories. Her writing has been published in a variety of places including the Narrative Travel Writing Contest online magazine; Transition Abroad's

2014 Narrative Travel Writing Contest awarded third place, and the ABC 360 documentary pocket doc stories.

Anita lives in Sydney and is currently working on a Memoir *My Life with Eggbert* (thirty-three years with one breast, after cancer); a middle grade novel and short stories. In between, she creates artworks, looks after grandsons and her garden, aided by Phoebe the cat and two hens, Ginger and Opal.

Anita has always been a storyteller (member of the NSW Storytellers Guild). As she writes, Anita finds it exciting to feel her characters come alive; exploring and interrelating with their surroundings and each other. She enjoys scrolling through alternative words suggested by a thesaurus, finding a possible 'word' and, like a pair of shoes, trying it within the sentence to see if it fits or clashes with tone or subtext.

KYLIE THOMPSON, is a writer and reviewer with a love of fictional mayhem. When she isn't reviewing movies and events for *Scenestr*, or books for a wealth of publications including *Reviewers of Oz* and *Hush Hush Biz,* she can be found scribbling  in notebooks, plotting the perfect fictional crimes. A love of pop culture and a frustration at negative tropes around mental illness in the works she adores pushed her towards a degree in Creative and Professional Writing, and a love of crime writing.

She is currently writing a dystopian crime series set in Brisbane, and more poetry than a crime writer would generally admit to. Kylie attended the 2015 and 2017 Rainforest Writers Retreats, and is incredibly proud to be a part of the inaugural RWR anthology.

You can follow Kylie's crime (writing) spree,
or just enjoy her ramblings, at
reviewersofoz.wordpress.com/ *and*
writerlyscrawls.wordpress.com/

Acknowledgements

Rainforest
Writing Retreat

RWR would like to thank Charmaine Clancy, Anthony Puttee and Chris Radge for their hard work in assembling this Anthology and also the warm staff of O'Reilly's who always treat us more like family rather than customers. Likewise, thanks are also due to the RWR retreaters/ authors, without whose work there wouldn't be a book. A big thanks to all the crew at the Self-publishing Lab previously known as Book Cover Café for the fantastic cover layout, editing, typesetting and everything else you do. You can contact them at www.selfpublishinglab.com

And the biggest thanks to Charmaine who thought that a writing retreat would be a great idea and has run with it ever since.

SELF-PUBLISHING AND MARKETING YOUR BOOK JUST GOT SIMPLER

selfpublishinglab.com

Online **Classroom**

The Lab is packed with in-depth, step-by-step practical video lessons, tools and resources on preparing, producing, publishing and promoting your book. PLUS the 24/7 community and coaching you need to ensure you achieve your full potential and goals.

Book **Creation**

Let us take care of these one-off tasks, so you can avoid any headaches. Our team is ready when you are. The Lab is an award-winning one-stop shop for creating and publishing a quality book with a team of professionals who care. Oh, and you'll have fun doing it too!

Book **Marketing & Coaching**

From Amazon Ads, building email lists to selling at tradeshows, the Lab has you covered. With courses, templates and our online community, all your questions can be answered with the support of the Lab team and other like-minded authors achieving their goals, just like you.

About the **Self-publishing Lab**

The Lab is an award-winning publishing destination helping thousands of writers avoid the traps in publishing and get started on the right foot.

With over 25 years in the publishing industry, Anthony and the team at the Self-publishing Lab continue to help authors become bestsellers, sell thousands of dollars worth of books online, at schools, workshops and to organisations.

Here's what makes the **Self-publishing Lab different**

- **No contracts or exclusive agreements** that sell your soul. You'll keep 100% royalties and control without it costing you an arm and a leg to publish your book.

- **We show you how to use technology to sell more books** while you sleep, even if you're a tech newbie.

- **Have your book distributed** and available for purchase online around the world, at bookstores and libraries in print and e-book.

Contact Us Today

 w: selfpublishinglab.com
e: support@selfpublishinglab.com

 PO BOX 187
Browns Plains, QLD
Australia, 4118

www.ingramcontent.com/pod-product-compliance
Lightning Source LLC
Chambersburg PA
CBHW021427110726
47901CB00008B/2326